BROTHERS-IN-ARMS

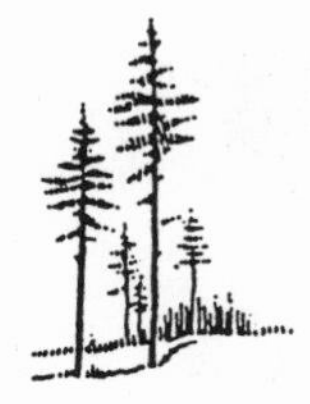

Also by Margaret Abbey
in Thorndike Large Print®

Francesca
The Flight of the Kestrel
Amber Promise

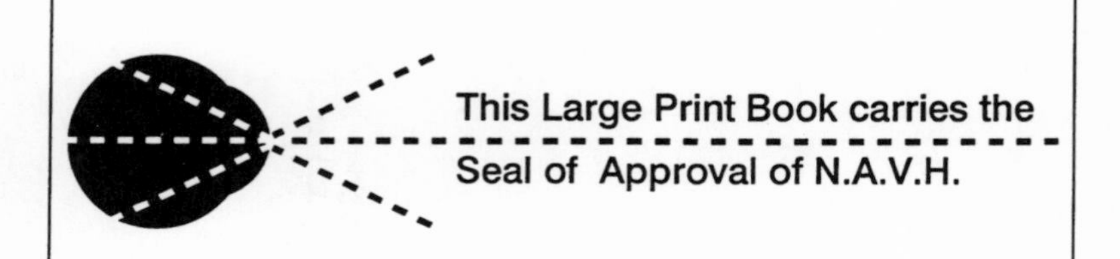

BROTHERS-IN-ARMS

Margaret Abbey

Thorndike Press • Thorndike, Maine

Library of Congress Cataloging in Publication Data:

Abbey, Margaret.
Brothers-in-arms / Margaret Abbey.
p. cm.
ISBN 1-56054-426-0 (alk. paper : lg. print)
1. Large type books. I. Title.
[PR6051.B28B7 1993] 92-43164
823'.914—dc20 CIP

Thorndike Large Print® Romance Series edition published in 1993 by arrangement with Margaret York.

Cover photo by Thayer Smith.

The tree indicium is a trademark of Thorndike Press.

This book is printed on acid-free, high opacity paper. ♾

DEDICATION

For Eileen Evison and Richard Blackburn who went with me to Tewkesbury Abbey and to Bloody Meadow.

Loyaulte me Lie.

AUTHOR'S NOTE

The characters of Catherine Newberry and Hugh Kingsford and the members of their families and households are fictitious, although a Sir William Newberry was among those executed after the battle of Tewkesbury in 1471. All other persons and events in the story are based on historical records.

PROLOGUE

May 1471

"Why, it's naught but a little maid, Wat. Let the child pass."

The archer struggled for some moments more while his comrade-in-arms watched him, grinning, and at last gave up the fight for mastery and released his prisoner.

The child fell back into the dust of the highway panting and sobbing with suppressed fear and fury. The man who had spoken reached down his hand to pull her to her feet. He was not prepossessing of appearance and she shrank from him.

"I'll not harm you, lass," he said gruffly, and, at last, she allowed him to help her.

She stood, head down, refusing to look at him and then she reached up tentative fingers to push back her hair, long and fair, which had streamed free from her hood when the two archers had barred her path and forced her to dismount from her pony. It was not surprising they had mistaken her for some page riding to the battlefield with a message. Determined to reach the field without hindrance she had ransacked Edmund's apartments for some garments more fitting her need. Edmund was her father's squire. Even now the lad fought with him in this bitter struggle for the languishing hopes of Lancaster. He was taller and broader than Catherine but she had found a doublet and hose he had long outgrown and donned them hastily. She could not enter Tewkesbury alone and in her girl's attire. Even she, desperately determined as she was, knew that.

The man addressed as Wat regarded him sourly. "Maid or no, we've orders to allow none to proceed from the Gloucester road. Best go back, lass, from wherever you came."

"The battle — ? My father fights for the Queen. How goes it?" Catherine addressed her question to the kinder of her jailers.

He shook his head and she shuddered as she noted the mud on his livery, and the more ominous dark brown stains that marked hose and leathern jacket. A sword cut had laid open one cheek from cheek-bone to chin, and the blood had congealed on the gash. It did not appear to concern him.

"York is triumphant, mistress, the Queen's cause lost."

Catherine swayed on her feet. "You — you are for York?"

"Aye, mistress, of Gloucester's company.

Our Duke drove the enemy back towards the river. Many drowned in the mill stream." Pitying her weakness for he saw she was near to collapse, he put out an arm to support her. She stepped backwards in an effort to evade him, moved clumsily and fell. He sank down by the roadside to lift her to his knee.

"Wat, have you some wine? The lass is faint."

The other, younger man, less villainous in appearance but more hostile in attitude, grudgingly handed over a half-emptied wine-skin.

Catherine shook her head appealingly but the archer coaxed her to swallow.

"Lass, you've no call to be here. Surely you came not with the army women?"

She did not answer and he bit his lip. "Do you live close by? You must go home and wait for news."

She turned her head from him to hide her tears.

"Don't you know, child, that the men in the town are overexcited?" He groped hesitantly for words to explain himself. "You'll not be safe, a little lass like you. How old are you, no more than ten, I'll be bound?"

Again she made no answer and he looked up at his fellow archer doubtfully. "Should we take her in charge for her own protection?"

"Nay, let her go her way. She'll not heed you. There'll be hundreds like her. You can't burden yourself with a child. We may be ordered to march by morning. What then?"

The older man turned his attention once more to the child. "Will you not go home? The pony will be stolen from you and you harmed. You cannot aid your father, lass. If he's slain naught can mend it; if taken, you must hope for the King's mercy."

She thrust out a stubborn chin. "I'll seek for his body."

"Nay, lass, that you will not." He pulled her to her feet determinedly. "The field's no place for you. Those that steal from the dead will cut your throat as soon as look on you. Go home and wait. Does your mother know you are from home?"

"My mother is dead long since. My nurse will be worried but that cannot be helped. I'll not go back without news of my father."

"There's some that took refuge in the Abbey." The archer looked down at her gravely. "If he lives he may well be with Somerset."

"And the Lord Prince Edward?" She sought for some crumb of comfort. Her father would be near the Prince if he yet lived.

Her informant looked to his comrade who shrugged.

"The Prince is slain, little maid, and My Lord Wenlock. 'Tis said Somerset slew him with his own hand. Why, God knows? Mayhap he feared Wenlock withheld his men from aiding the Duke. The Prince's body is taken to the Abbey, the Queen and her ladies fled towards Oxford. I treat you as a full-grown maid. I spare you nothing for I see that you are stout of heart, but there is naught you can do. You must see that. Let me put you back on your pony and you must ride home. The King will take no action against maids and children. In time he will order your estate. Your father may come home. Now, be a good maid and do what is best for him. If he comes home in two or three days and finds you gone, will he then be comforted? Believe me you help him best by taking our counsel." He grinned crookedly. "If you knew aught of the world you'd know you are fortunate to fall in with us and not others of our company. I've a maid of my own at home, aye and a babe of a lad too. I'd not see you spoiled." He tilted up her chin and looked hard at her. "Do you know what I mean?"

She swallowed hard and nodded. She was no babe. She knew well enough what soldiers did to captive women, even sometimes to children like herself, though she was not yet eleven and had not had her first show of blood which Arlette her nurse told her would proclaim her a woman.

Wat growled in his friend's ear. "We'll be relieved soon. God's teeth, Ralf, let the maid be. If she's for the town let her pass." He gave a rough guffaw. "She can scarce harm the King's cause."

Ralf was not convinced. "She'll harm her own. If she runs free in the town she'll not go home again, or if she does —" He left the rest unsaid.

Wat ran a hand through his cropped hair, lifted clear his salet to scratch his itching poll.

"I tell you, here's our relief. I'm for the camp. Let these two argue with the lass."

Ralf hesitated as his comrade went to greet the two archers reporting for guard duty.

"You'd be safe in the Abbey precincts. You may find your father there or get news of him. Swear you'll not leave the grounds or the church's protection and I'll see you safe to the Abbey door."

Impulsively she stooped and kissed his hand. He withdrew it awkwardly. It stank of leather and sweat and had done ill deeds today. She had no cause to treat it thus, but obviously she had decided. It was the best security he could hope for her. While Wat waited, sardonically, he lifted her to the pony's back and urged her forward towards Tewkesbury.

The archer was right. The victorious Yorkist soldiery had run riot in the town. Those townfolks who had respect for lives and property had stayed close in their own homes, boarding up doorways and windows against marauders. Taverns had been broken into and men reeled drunkenly across roads, not heeding baggage wagons, carts and mounted knights and squires impatiently sent on errands by their respective masters. An angry bellow of rage was frequently levelled at some shrieking fool who tore in pursuit of a helpless, sobbing girl and impeded the passage of a noble lord. Men were already loading weapons, salets, jacks, boots, drinking cups, anything of value looted from the field into carts or breaking into some cottage where the booty could be hidden until the army was given the order to march once more.

Catherine shrank terrified against the burly form of her archer companion. Wat had already forsaken them for more pleasurable company. Ralf halted the pony and gave her a crooked grin of comfort.

"Soon we'll be at the Abbey door. Keep up your spirits, lass. Is your father yeoman, or gentleman?"

"He is a knight baronet, Sir Wilfred Newberry of Newburgh Manor, three miles this side of Gloucester. We are related to the Newburghs of Lulworth in Dorset."

"Are there brothers?"

"No, my father's squire, Edmund Tollerton, is with him. These are Edmund's clothes."

"I see."

"You think he is less likely to survive." She leaned forward, clutching at his hand on the bridle rein.

He was anxious to spare her, yet this child could not be lied to convincingly.

"Lesser folk will more easily escape the field. 'Tis not to be denied, lass. The King will try the rebels. He is not vindictive, our glorious Ned —"

"My father is no rebel. He fights for his rightful King, Harry of Lancaster." Despite her childish shrillness, she was firm enough in her defence of him.

"Aye, lass, I'll not dispute the rights of the matter with you. I but fight for my own lord and he is in Gloucester's household. Now here we are. You must walk the rest of the way. The crowd round the Abbey door is too dense. I'll take your pony round to the Abbey stables and try to find some place for him. I warn you, you're like to lose him."

She nodded impatiently as he lifted her down.

"Mingle with the crowd. Those knights who escaped the field have claimed Sanctuary, though God knows for how long. You may find your father among them. I pray you do, little lass. Your courage deserves a reward."

She reached up and impulsively hugged him. "The Virgin bless you and bring you safe home." She tugged at a ring on her finger. "Give this your own girl. Tell her how you helped Catherine Newberry, though she is your enemy."

He held the tiny thing in his bloodstained hand. "You've no need to reward me, child, but I will take it to remind me of a brave lass. If ever I can help you —" He broke off awkwardly.

Her voice carried a quaint dignity, of some stately dame, small, ill-clad and dishevelled as she was. "I understand you well. Our estate will be forfeit and our family disgraced. We shall face it if God is merciful and my father wins through. Our time will come. What is your name?"

"Ralf Bradman in the service of Sir Hugh Kingsford. I come from Cadeby in the county of Leicestershire."

She started and he eyed her curiously. Some movement of the crowd thrust her violently against him and he lost the gist of some of what she said.

"The Kingsfords are related —"

He steadied her and she thanked him gravely.

"Go now, Ralf Bradman. It may go hard with you if you are seen helping the child of an enemy."

He laughed out loud. "Lass, who'll know you're friend or foe, but I must go about my duties. Squeeze through and get you into the Abbey and mind your promise. You'll not leave its walls until the violence has quietened down. The monks will keep you safe."

He watched her, frowning anxiously till she was lost from view among the crowd of the more courageous townsfolk who had flocked to the Abbey door to watch the bearers of the Prince's body pass to the sanctified peace of the chancel.

Catherine forced her way through despite the any expletives launched at her. The front of the crowd curved in a curious half circle round the North porch, drawing back as the officials of the Abbey passed through into the Nave. There were no guards and no one appointed to prevent entry into the Church and Catherine scrambled forward and ran up the gravel pathway and came to a breathless halt with one hand on the great door. She could hear nothing from inside. The stone and massive weight of the door effectively cut off all sound. She pushed experimentally expecting that some barrier might now have been erected to stop more fugitives from seeking sanctuary but the door opened easily and she passed into the sudden chill of the great church.

The noise met her immediately, the terrible sound of mourning, sobs and wailing from the chancel where the bodies of the noble slain had been placed, choking coughs and groans from the nave itself, now crowded with the press of the fugitives, many wounded, some crying shamelessly in pain supported by comrades whose hopeless expressions showed the futility of their struggle to this place. What safety there was, could be only of short duration. The victorious King would demand that the rebel survivors be given up to his officers. It could only be a matter of time but for the moment they were safe to rest and lick their wounds, even gather their remnants of courage, it was enough. They ignored her entrance, her passage amongst them. She felt it would be useless to ask any for news of her father. Each seemed intent upon his own wretchedness with the exception of those who tried vainly to give assistance to some wounded companion. Lords, knights, squires, pikemen, archers, they all crept together, for once achieving a measure of equality in their need to seek protection from the Sanctuary of the Great Rood on the High Altar.

It was gloomy under the great soaring arches and the faces of the men unrecognizable, besmirched with blood and filth. Some knelt before the Rood Screen sobbing out prayers and Catherine drew back as she saw the bier which had been placed there. She could not see the face of the young Prince, seventeen years old, the last hope of the House of Lancaster. Someone had hastily covered the slight armoured form with a cloak and the tatters of a standard. Catherine shivered uncontrollably. Was the young face disfigured, the boy's form smashed and hacked by mace and battle-axe? She had heard one whisper that the Prince had fallen from his destrier and been ridden down by the pursuing Yorkist lords.

"Poor lad," the woman had sobbed, "they say he's unrecognizable except for the gold chain round his neck and the rich chasing of the armour. Who'll comfort the Queen and poor mad Harry, his father?"

Monks were already lighting the tall candles about the bier and chanting the offices for the dead. She knelt herself and prayed fervently for the soul of the young Prince, all those slain and that she might find her father and Edmund among the survivors.

It took what seemed an age to circle the nave, peering into weary, dispirited faces, pleading for news from one or two who seemed less sunken in their own sorrow. She was answered by silent shakes of the head or sad verbal refusals. No one knew if her father was yet alive and she found none who were personally known to her. Wearily she was prepared to acknowledge defeat and sank down on the stone floor, near the North door, tears beginning to trickle through the fingers covering her face. She had promised the Yorkist archer, Ralf, that she would not leave the Abbey sanctuary and for the moment she had not the strength or the courage to do so.

Suddenly the great door was thrust open and the clamour from the town reached the ears of those in the nave. Shouting, the jingle of accoutrements, the ring of armour. Men moved from the proximity of the porch in an effort to seek the greater safety of the High Altar. Catherine found herself jerked to her feet and pulled with them.

"Move back, lad, the Yorkist lords intend to break Sanctuary."

"No," she whispered, "no one would do that, not even Edward of March."

"Lad, the King is the King. He is hot with the heady wine of victory. I doubt that even the Abbot will say him nay."

The man did not appear to note her sex. Already he had lost interest in her and was intent on saving his own skin. For the first time she realized how desperate was her own position. If what the man said was true, the Lancastrian knights were trapped here and could be butchered as easily as sheep in a pen.

She slipped in a pool of blood and would have been crushed underfoot had not another man stooped to seize her by the hand.

"Up, child. Fall now and you're doomed."

She clutched at his mailed hand gratefully and pulled herself up. He looked over her boy's clothing curiously.

"You're over-young for the fight. Which knight brought a child so young to the field? Surely you are page still and no squire." He started, bent and lifted up her chin. "You're a lass. Deny it not."

She gulped, finding herself forced against the cold steel of his corselet.

"I'm Catherine Newberry. I seek my father."

"In the name of God, child, you did ill. You can do him no service here." He pointed. "Look, Edward himself with Gloucester and Clarence."

There were the sounds of clashing armour from near the door, a stifled scream as some unfortunate man was drawn through the door and dealt with summarily. Catherine looked fearfully at the intruders.

The King made a glorious terrifying sight in his gilded armour, dented and stained, the crown of England encircling his helm. His mailed hand flourished his drawn sword. So this was Edward of March, eldest son of Richard of York, self-styled King of England since the Battle of Mortimer's Cross. Three suns had miraculously appeared in the sky, they said, heralding victory for the young Earl, vengeance for the bloody work at Wakefield. That sun had now become his personal device, the Sun in Splendour. Frightened as she was, Catherine could see he was a splendid giant of a man, dwarfing the two Princes who stood by his side. It was clear to see who was the King.

The man on the King's right was puny by comparison, his own gilded armour gleaming under the faint light of mass candles kindled by some knight who prayed for the soul of a dead comrade. He wielded a battle-axe, but abruptly put up his weapon, gesturing to another lord on the far side of the King to do likewise. The other, taller lord shook his head. Like the King and the other prince he had raised his visor showing a florid, handsome face and traces of red-golden hair, thrust back from his helm. He moved forward aggressively, stooping to peer into the faces of those nearest, as if to identify some personal enemy.

"My Lord King." The clear ringing tones from the vicinity of the altar caused the King to raise his sword, halting the knights behind him who were still engaged in dragging out those wounded they could reach.

From the chancel came the dignified tall figure of the Abbot Strensham, holding high the Holy Chalice. He had been celebrating Mass and he was clad in his embroidered vestments.

"My Lord King, will you deny the protection of Holy Mother Church and allow your followers to defile this sanctified place? Order your men to cease from slaughter. I charge you to do so in the name of our most merciful Saviour."

The King's raised sword had already signalled his intent to heed the Abbot's words. He lowered it and stood leaning on the hilt. There was a sudden hush.

When he spoke it was with a beauty and dignity as challenging as the voice of the Abbot.

"Will you allow these foul rebels to escape the justice of the realm by crawling here and clinging to the robes of monks? They have taken up arms against their anointed sovereign. Will you deny that, Father Abbot?"

"I deny nothing, My Lord. I am a son of Holy Church. I take no part in the wars of Princes but these men have sought sanctuary and by the laws of that church I serve, I must grant it."

"Must?" The fair lord who stood on the left of the King strode forward impatiently. "Who says 'must' to Edward the King? Who will protect you, old man, or your monks if we sweep into this church and slay all rebels who cowardly cling together here instead of facing us bravely in the open country?"

The King checked this outburst with a gesture of contempt.

"Peace, George. The Abbot speaks with the authority of his office. However," he looked round grimly, "I am by no means satisfied that my enemies should be allowed to escape me. For the good of the realm, Father Abbot, these insurgents must be brought to trial, this business must be settled once and for all."

The smaller Prince said quietly, "These men cannot remain within the Abbey for ever, Father Abbot. What, then, do you suggest?"

The old man's eyes regarded him fearlessly. "My Lord of Gloucester, you speak wisely. I cannot protect these men when they leave the shelter of the Abbey, nor, I hasten to add, do I wish to do so, if they are as you say, truly traitors to the realm. I ask only that they may this night stay within the church, tend their wounded and pray for the souls of the dead. In common humanity, I ask the King to grant this."

The King considered. Angry murmurs came from the men behind him.

"It is well, Father Abbot. We will withdraw. I grant these men until tomorrow, then they must of their own will come forth from the Church to face judgement, particularly I demand the person of Edmund Beaufort, Duke of Somerset."

A man rose from his knees near the bier of the dead Prince and came to the entrance of the Rood Screen.

"I expect no mercy, Edward of March. Though I walk to my death, I will come through the door of the North porch at first light to meet my judges."

"Still you refuse to afford me the courtesy of my true title, King of England."

"I do not recognize your right," the man's voice drooped with weakness. "Harry of Lancaster is my King and he only do I serve, now that his heir is slain. Now, leave me with my dead."

The King's grip on his sword hilt trembled. For a second Catherine thought he might yet defy the authority of the Abbot and strike down his enemy, there before the altar, then he nodded, turned and strode back towards the great door, his nobles giving way before him.

In the porch, the taller Prince, Catherine now knew to be George of Clarence, stopped and walked round the back of the huge pillar which fronted the door. Stooping, he peered into the face of a wounded man who was slumped against its base. He said no word but at length returned to his royal brother who had paused, awaiting him in the doorway. The King's face was reddened with anger and his hand on his hip in a gesture of exaggerated politeness.

"Well, brother," he said icily, "may we proceed? We wait on your leisure."

Clarence muttered some apology then bowed for his elder brother to precede him. As they went Catherine thought she heard him say clearly one word only in a hurried sentence of explanation. "Newberry" then almost smothered by the clank of armour, "I thought as much. Warwick —"

She waited transfixed till they were gone, the King and his suite, the massive door clanging shut behind them, then she gathered her failing strength and stumbled to the rear of the pillar.

The man who had attracted the Duke's attention wearily lifted his head, his eyes dully regarding the new intruder. Catherine's hungry eyes flashed over him. He had removed his helm and a blood-stained kerchief bound his brow. One arm hung limply and his mouth was held in a tight line of pain. All the vivacity had drained from the face with its normal healthy colour. The whole body seemed denuded of the very life-force itself, but she had no doubts. She gave a little choking cry and held out her arms, sinking to her knees in a mute gesture of greeting.

He continued to stare, then the eyes blazed in a sudden glory and he struggled to pull himself upright.

"Catherine, my Catherine." It was clear that for the moment he could not believe the evidence of his own eyes. Surely what he saw was a vision, no flesh and blood child here in this bloody shambles, the remnant of a defeated army.

She ran to press herself close, warm tears raining on to his hand free from the mailed gauntlet. She was real enough. He could feel her, smell the sweetness of her tumbled hair, press his lips on the little hand that reached up to gauge the serious nature of his head wound.

He clutched her to his heart with his uninjured arm, crooning to her in an excess of delight, heightened rather than lessened by the shock of finding her here. At last his fears for her won through the joy of his discovery. He put back her head with a gentle hand looking into her tear-drenched grey eyes.

"Catherine, my love, my heart, what are you going here? Did not Arlette keep you safe as I bade her?" Another fear caused a pulse to beat fast in his temple. "York's soldiers — they have not reached the manor. You —"

"No," she reassured him quickly. "I am at fault. I had to look for you. I could not bear the waiting. Edmund —"

He avoided her eyes, stroking the straggling silk of her hair. "He fell early when Gloucester attacked. I have heard no news of him since. We must believe the boy lost. During the pursuit in that bloody meadow he would have been crushed underfoot. We cannot hope, Catherine. It is better so."

"And you, are you badly hurt? Your head, your arm —"

"The arm received a blow from an axe, the head wound is not serious, though it aches as if some imp of hell was tormenting me with red-hot hammers. I shall do well enough."

He smoothed back her hair and cupped her chin in his hand.

"What of you? You are now my principal concern. You cannot leave the Abbey while those Yorkish pikemen and bowmen sack the town. You must stay here tonight." He paused, bit his lip and went on doggedly. "Afterwards, after I have surrendered myself, you must throw yourself on the protection of the Abbot. Go to the almonry. They will care for you until the town is quiet."

She lay curled up against him for the rest of that night. There was nothing she could do for him. Monks tended those most gravely wounded and some wine was handed round. The Abbot knew well he would further enrage the King if he made food and supplies available to the rebels and contented himself with granting only necessities. Catherine felt no pangs of hunger though she had eaten nothing all day and very little yesterday; her anxiety had been too great. At last she slept, though she had struggled to remain awake.

A gentle pressure on her shoulder roused her. She was stiff and cold on the stone floor though curled against her father. Grey light was filtering only dimly through the upper clerestory windows. The chanting of the monks came faintly from the chancel. She heard the mutter of lowered voices as around her men were being shriven.

She shuddered and reached for her father's hand.

"I must seek a priest, child. Stay here till

I come back to you."

Her eyes widened in sudden fear and he reassured her gently.

"It is likely the King will be merciful. I am no noble lord. If God is good he may exact a heavy fine or confiscate our land. Times will be hard, child, but —"

"Nothing matters if you are safe."

She prayed herself while he went from her to his confession. The stone struck chill through the wool of Edmund's hose to her knees. It was May. It would soon be high summer. God grant they all be happy again soon except for Edmund's mother. Poor Lady Jane, she would weep for many months yet —

Somerset had come down from the chancel and gathered his knights around him.

"Gentlemen," he said quietly, "soon we must keep our word and go out with the dawn. I pray you all to make your peace with God and to have a good courage. I shall ask of the King's mercy to allow the Prince's body to be buried within the Abbey precincts, aye and the bodies of those of our number already dead. I am informed the Queen and the Princess of Wales were captured by a detachment of Clarence's men. I do not expect the King to be harsh with Queen Margaret. It is likely she will join our good King Harry in the Tower. You will note that I speak of Edward of March as our King. Those of you who receive the mercy of the King, and God grant it will be many of you, must now accept him as such. Warwick the Kingmaker's death at Barnet sealed our hopes. They lie with our young Prince there." He indicated the draped bier. "Those of you who live must decide your own allegiance. Young Henry Tudor is in exile. It may be, in time, he may revive the Lancastrian claim though his birth is not such to warrant this. Each of you will consider your own conscience in this matter. If you can aid the Queen in aught I plead with you now to do so." He looked round the circle of men who had drawn close to hear his final orders. "Knights will ask mercy for their squires. All must leave the Abbey now. Our word to the Lord Abbot must be honoured."

Catherine's father returned to her side. He put a comforting arm round her shoulder. "We shall go out together. I shall request protection for you from some knight. You must not be afraid."

She conquered her tears. "I will not show fear and I will do what you ask. Come to the almonry for me." Her whisper was pitiful and he stooped and kissed her chilled brow.

The long shuffle from the Abbey Church seemed to take an age. Catherine watched her father's face anxiously but he showed no sign of pain. Like the others his face was drawn and pale in the grey morning light, but he seemed more confident now that the fate of each of them would soon be known.

At the door stood two Yorkist knights. Their faces were strange to her. Efficiently they herded their prisoners with the assistance of a company of halberdiers. The common soldiers, archers, pikemen and squires were allowed to go free after leaving all weapons at the Church door. The King had granted them their liberty. They hastened off, melting into the morning mists without backward glances at their less fortunate superiors. Knights and older squires of the body were marched off under guard to the King's camp, Catherine's father among them.

The Duke of Somerset, the Prior of St. John, Sir Thomas Tresham, Sir Gervase Clifton and some dozen other men Catherine had heard her father name were kept under strict guard and marched into the town.

Catherine's father had whispered urgently with the knight who asked in clipped cold tones his name and station. The man waved away the youngster impatiently and she stood aside until she could no longer see the little procession which held her father within its midst, then stumbled, white-faced, to the Abbey almonry.

The great long room was packed solid with those patiently waiting for the monks' charity. Now at last she was spent and stood tiredly against the wall until a youthful monk offered her dark bread, cheese, and a cup of ale. She thanked him quietly and when the others dispersed remained where she was. The young monk, though eyeing her curiously, indicated a rough wooden bench where she might rest herself and left her.

The hours passed and the monks returned with more food as yet more of the town's poor came expectantly for alms. Catherine ate what she received and it strengthened her, though it seemed tasteless. Throughout the hours of daylight she remained obediently within the Abbey grounds. Surely, now, her father would come for her.

When dark fell the place was dimly illumined with two tallow dips. The young monk who gave alms came to the door of the almonry. There were five people only, an old man who sat at the far end of the bench, mumbling foolishly and dribbling into his beard, a family of displaced yeomen, or so Catherine supposed since the man loudly protested the King's right to seize his farm, commandeer his cattle and hens, and allow his archers to pursue his daughter. His wife entreated him tearfully to desist, whispering that when the King's men had left the town they would be able to return and put right some of the damage. The daughter, a robust girl of some fourteen years, sat sulkily silent as if she regretted her sire's determination to drag her with him to the security of the Abbey. The remaining guest was an elderly archer who had come to seek treatment for his injured arm, which hung useless by his side. He munched the hard bread without comment and Catherine wondered if he would ever again engage in his trade. He was clearly a paid mercenary and his sword arm was now useless, indeed later, he might lose it if the crushed bone and muscle failed to heal.

He watched her more carefully than the others and she moved abruptly further off.

"You'll be body squire to a Lancastrian knight," he said at last, "else you'd be about your business in the King's camp."

She cleared her throat, husky with unshed tears. "I came with my father, Sir Wilfred Newberry. I'm waiting for him to be freed so that he can fetch me."

He spat on the mud floor. "All knights and body squires not arraigned for judgement were freed long since. Are you sure your father lives?"

She went cold with horror. "But my father

was not taken with My Lord Somerset. Are you sure — ?"

"Aye, I'm sure. 'Tis said sixteen lords and knights are to be tried tomorrow at first light by the Lord High Constable, young Gloucester, the King's brother, and the Earl Marshal. They are accused of double treason, having given previous allegiance to York. It's not likely that any will be proved innocent. They're erecting a gallows in the market place."

"But my father is no great lord. He fought for the Queen today for the first time because he truly pitied her. He has never intrigued against the King."

The archer spat again. "Someone'll have borne him a grudge mayhap, sworn false evidence."

"But why? Who hates my father — ?"

He shrugged. "You'll have land. Are there sons to inherit?"

She shook her head, dry-mouthed, not even conscious that he had recognized her girlhood at last.

He lifted his ale-cup gingerly with his uninjured hand. "I can see now, you're a lass. Best hide here till it's all over, one way or the other." He nodded towards the farmer's wife. "Sleep over there, near her. No one will molest you."

"Sleep?" Catherine scrambled towards the door. "I must find where they've taken my father, plead for him, make them listen —"

"Not now, child, the Abbey gates are fast locked. You can do nothing. You'll not even find him. Stay until morning. It may be not as I said. He may have been delayed."

This rough attempt at comfort having little effect, he gave his concentration to the difficult task of eating lefthanded.

She sprang up and tried the door. It was as he'd said, barred. She knew it would be useless to battle against it, since the monks would now be at supper and later at divine office in the Chapel. No one would hear her. Somehow she must wait through these terrible dark hours until she could leave the Abbey and enquire of her father's fate in the town.

The sun was high by the time Catherine won free from the Abbey almonry. She had waited in an agony for the doors to be unbarred the moment she saw light steal into the long bare room through a small horn window high up on the far wall. The wounded archer had snored throughout the night, as had the farmer and his wife. The girl had woken once to flounce up into a sitting position but she was too close to her mother to attempt to draw nearer either Catherine or the archer, so she'd given a heavy sigh and snuggled down again into the partially clean straw. The young monk again brought food and Catherine appealed to him to unbar the main gate. He was sorry to refuse her but he had not the authority to order the porter to do so and he urged her to eat.

As a line of paupers came patiently to the Abbey gate Catherine forced her way through and made for the market square. Here in the street she found her way again barred. A crowd had gathered to watch the executions in the market square.

Catherine was desperate. It could not yet be so late. Surely the trials would still be proceeding. The stolid bystanders good-naturedly refused to give ground for her. She coaxed, commanded, pleaded. Not one of them would budge. One big man, by the greasy smell of him and the blood marks on his jerkin, a butcher, thrust a brawny arm across her chest.

"Whither so fast? If you wanted to see the show you should have risen earlier, young sir."

"Let me through, you fool. I must speak with the judges."

"Oh yes, young sprig," he mimicked. "The Lord High Constable, the most puissant Duke of Gloucester, Lord High Admiral of the Fleet, Warden of the Marches, will naturally give ear to what you have to say."

"Perhaps he's a personal friend of the Earl Marshal," one other wit mopped his eyes streaming with mirth at the youth's determination.

"Please," she panted, "I was in the Abbey. The gate was barred. My father is accused. Let me through I beg you."

A country woman in bright red kirtle, thrust the butcher aside. "God's mercy, man, let the boy pass. Can't you see he's distressed."

The butcher's face became grave. "Wife, it will ill become me to let him see this, if we do."

He cleared a space round the reeling child. "The executions are begun, child. You'll not want to watch, not if you've kinsfolk among the condemned."

The world went black for one split second. The kindly woman supported her thin shoulders. She felt deadly sick. She heard a sudden excited rustle ahead, a heavy thud and a great sigh from the crowd. The woman stooped and put a hand on her hair.

"It's quick, they say. No one's to be quartered. Go and wait near the Abbey till it's over."

It would be simple now to give it all up and go. If her father were condemned she could do nothing. She was terribly afraid. Her bowels had turned to water and the bile rose in her throat. She could not watch. It would not be expected. He would not wish it. He had never in his whole life spoken of an execution before her. He had shielded her from the thought, though he must have seen several. She wavered as the woman urged her gently to the back of the crowd. Then she knew she could not fail him now. She must try to get close, if he still lived, to see him.

She clawed at the woman's hand. "I — I must try to see him."

The woman peered down at her, pity apparent on her fat, honest face.

"Will," she said giving her man a heavy push, "get the lad to the front. You can do it, you big ox."

He grunted objection then catching her eye, he nodded and thrust a brawny arm between the two smaller men over whose shoulder he peered.

"Make way, friends. Here's one whose need is pressing."

They turned to argue but he caught Catherine by the arm and forced her in front of him. So great was his girth that grumbling and cursing, the crowd gave way before him until Catherine's way was barred by crossed pikes.

"Back, lad, no further," one of the men warned.

She fell against the cold steel then stumbled to her feet.

Before her was the market square cleared of the townsfolk. On a dais some distance from her she saw two elegantly clad figures seated on wooden armchairs. The smaller of the two she recognized though he wore no armour today. Richard of Gloucester, the King's younger brother, was clad in a doublet and hose of sober hue. She saw the gold chain he wore gleam in the sunlight. He was bare-headed and his brown hair seemed lighter, almost bronze in the light, touched with the red-gold glints of his two fairer brothers. From here she could not catch the expression on his face, though he sat bolt-upright not leaning towards or talking with the older, more burly man seated by his side. Norfolk had also chosen to wear a sober garment of some dark green cloth, fur-trimmed for the distasteful task of the morning.

Unwillingly Catherine forced her gaze to the scaffold. Already the straw was slippery with blood and the headsman, bare-armed, a leather apron covering jerkin and hose, leaned wearily on the heavy handled axe. She could not look at two soldiers who had returned from carting off the latest corpse and had thrown sacking or coarse cloth over the pathetic heap near the far corner of the platform. From her right she heard the jingle of spurs, the strike of iron on the cobbles. Two guards marched the last prisoner forward. He walked without hesitation towards the steps then, turning and seeing her, stumbled. He held out one hand imploring her to turn away. His arm was seized by one of his guards and he was firmly but gently urged to the steps.

She could not take her eyes from his loved form. He was not allowed to speak to the crowd. She saw him say brief words to the executioner who nodded gravely. He had stumbled in the bloodied straw and the guard assisted him to the block. It was over very quickly as the woman said. He knelt as if at prayer. Catherine saw the upright gleam of the axe-head as it was lifted from the straw. Afterwards she wondered how silvery it shone in the sun, since it had already done bloody work that day. It descended with a terrible jarring thud. There was no cry, no sound from the doomed man, again a long sigh from those round the scaffold and it was done. Catherine sank down to her knees behind the crossed pikes. It seemed that everything in the world had stopped. She saw nothing, none of those about her, not the noble lords who rose now after this final execution, not the soldiers who piled the carcasses into the three or four carts driven in to receive them. When the pikes were withdrawn she stumbled to the scaffold steps, put her head on the straw and stayed there. She was too bewildered, too numbed to weep. There was no feeling in her. All she saw was her father's tall figure again mounting the steps, stooping to the headsman, stumbling, then kneeling.

She was only half aware of a movement by her. Dully she thought the soldiers would try to drag her away and she put out a hand to clutch at the rough wood of the improvised rail. A voice she had heard only once before, but one she would never forget, addressed a companion.

"Why do fools allow children to witness these sights?"

She felt a hand on her shoulder and tried to shake it off, but the grip was firm.

"Boy, you cannot stay here. If you are sick you should not be afraid to show it. It's natural enough."

She made no answer and his companion said curtly, "Stand up, boy. Answer His Grace of Gloucester."

Still she made no move and her captor stooped and drew her to her feet. She had tried to pin up her hair, knowing that if she were seen to be a girl men would try to prevent her reaching the market place; now it fell free about her shoulders and as he turned her to face him he gave an exclamation of shocked surprise.

"A girl, and younger than I supposed. Who brought you here, child?"

She stared up at him out of a face distorted with grief and hate.

"No one brought me, My Lord, I came to seek my father. I found him in time to see him die."

His face whitened and his companion moved involuntarily as if to prevent further impertinence. Gloucester made a commanding gesture of his free hand. His voice was grave but kindly.

"I am sorry."

"That he died or that I saw him?"

"Child, be silent." The knight moved to withdraw this child from the Duke's sight so distraught with grief that she did not know what she was saying or had not realized to whom she spoke, but the Duke answered her quietly.

"That you saw it, mistress. You are surely not alone in Tewkesbury. Is your mother in the town? Hugh, take charge of the lass and see her safe."

"My mother is dead."

The two men looked at each other blankly.

"Where is your home? Did you come with the Queen's Army?" The Duke was persistent.

She turned from him wearily. "The manor is three miles from Gloucester. My nurse is there but she can't help me now."

"By the Virgin, Hugh, this child is in sore straits. The estate is confiscate to the Crown. She cannot go back. The house may be sacked."

"Aye, sir. She will be in the King's charge. Perhaps if we were to place her under guard until we know his pleasure —"

"No." The Duke frowned. "The child needs care, not jailers. Bring her to my lodging."

"But, My Lord —"

"I'll take her to the nunnery at Gupshill. The nuns will treat her kindly. The Queen and the Lady Anne took refuge there during the battle. Surely they will treat this Lancastrian child well."

"I will go for you, sir."

Gloucester had released Catherine into the other's charge and moved slightly from them. He turned and gave a wry smile.

"Thank you, Hugh, but I have my own reasons for riding to Gupshill." He checked.

"Since I condemned her father I feel responsibility for this child, rightly or no. We'll question those who know her later."

Catherine would have resisted when the man, Hugh, attempted to follow the Duke, but she was so wearied with useless struggling against insurmountable odds and she staggered. Gloucester turned sharply and lifted her into his arms. She heard the other man demur but not the Duke's answer. Merciful nature took its toll at last and she slipped into unconsciousness.

She could not have recalled later what happened at the Duke's lodging. She must have regained consciousness but she was so lost to her own despair that she seemed unaware of those around her.

Her next waking thought was being held firmly against a man's body as he skilfully handled his mount, while supporting her with one arm. She stirred and he spoke quietly.

"Stay still, mistress. We shall soon be there."

Again she went white to the lips at the sound of that hated voice. Richard of Gloucester, Lord High Constable of England who had judged and condemned her father, while other men went free — what had he now in mind for her?

He drew rein and she heard muttered

voices. It was now growing late. A man's arms were stretched to lift her down and the Duke's voice came again.

"Gently now."

She waited near the archer as he set her carefully on her feet. The world seemed to whirl unaccountably. Lighted brands appeared to come from nowhere and dazzle her eyes. She put up a hand to thrust them off. Then she saw him looking gravely down at her. The brand illumined his youthful, clever face, the mouth held in as if he kept it tight lest it betrayed his own pain. He was frowning, though frightened as she was, she knew he was not angry with her.

Then abruptly he dropped to one knee before her, reaching up his hands to her slight, drooping shoulders.

"Child, listen to me and try to understand. Your father was a traitor. He was judged fairly and my duty was to condemn him. His end was clean and quick. I will see he is buried in sanctified ground in or near the Abbey. Will you trust me?"

Her eyes brimmed with sudden tears and she nodded.

"Tell me his name."

"Wilfred Newberry."

"Have you brothers?"

She shook her head and he gave a little sigh.

"I've brought you to Gupshill. The nuns will care for you. Be obedient and brave. You are in the King's charge now."

Anger returned and with it her spirit.

"I'd rather beg in the streets than trust to the good offices of His Grace the King, nor do I need your favours, My Lord of Gloucester."

He did not become angered though she thought he might have struck her. He continued to look at her gravely, then he rose and took her hand.

"Come."

The portress expressed concern at His Grace's charge, while she curtsied low to their distinguished visitor. She was not unaware that their house might well be held under the King's extreme displeasure. Had not Queen Margaret and Prince Edward's widow, the Kingmaker's daughter, and their ladies been sheltered here, and now this Yorkist Prince had come to call them to account.

In the Abbess's parlour Gloucester confronted the Convent's Superior. She, too, gaunt and pale with fear, was assiduous in her duty to His Grace. Catherine was left to stand dispiritedly near to the door, while the two conferred.

When the Duke left her again he placed one hand on her shoulder.

"The King will be informed, child. You would not enjoy to beg, I assure you. Mendicants are whipped at the cart's tail, as well you know. I leave you in charge of the Abbess. Mass shall be said for your father's soul."

She did not answer him and at last he was gone. Still she stood silent until a nun came to her side with a swish of her roughly woven habit across the rushes.

"Come, child, you are hungry and tired. First, let me take you to the infirmary. You need care for your hands."

Catherine looked down at them stupidly. She was vaguely surprised to find them raw and bleeding, the wrists and fingers badly scratched. She bad been unaware of pain and could not remember how the wounds had occurred. She looked up into the round, red face of the elderly woman, brow serene under the still whiteness of her coif and veil. Her brown eyes shone with pity for the bedraggled child whose eyes were dark with suffering. She held wide her arms. Catherine drew back for an instant then she allowed herself to be caught close to the nun's habit, her wooden beads hard against the child's dirt-streaked cheek. Then the tears came thick and fast. The older woman did not seek to check them. She hugged her charge tightly and at last drew her from the parlour towards the snug little infirmary where the convent sick were treated and cosseted. That was all the child needed now. The comfort of loving arms and understanding hearts, that, at least, they could give her.

CHAPTER I

March 1477

Catherine heard them calling soon after Matins. She made herself secure with her back snug against the elm trunk, drawing her grey kirtle tight round her legs lest it droop and betray her presence. The two youngest novices had circled the orchard calling, then meeting with little suppressed giggles at the futility of their efforts. Eventually they had returned to the convent to continue work on the new altar cloth for the Lady Chapel.

It was not that she disliked their company. They were pleasant natured girls, Joan from a farm near Worcester, Martha, older and almost ready for her final vows, a clerk's daughter from the Town. Martha was seventeen, Joan younger than herself, only last Martinmas turned fifteen. Catherine liked to be with them most days — not when the sun, unexpectedly warm, dappled the orchard with light and shade and from here, high in the tree, she could see the river glinting silver in the distance. If she turned her back the lantern tower of the Abbey Church would dominate over ploughed land; below the warm red brick of the Convent living quarters and the Lady Chapel of more sombre grey stone.

It was a small foundation of fourteen nuns under the Abbess and six novices. The rule of the Abbess was firm but gentle and the older nuns rarely squabbled amongst themselves as in many larger houses where ambition was rife among the sisterhood.

The work had been hard but they had loved her, from the Mother herself to the meanest scullion who worked in the kitchen under the cheerful but imperious rule of Sister Marie Joseph. Though she had shared the simple fare of the sisters and went dressed demurely she had no complaints regarding her welfare. She had been as well educated as any daughter of an Earl. She could read and write a fair hand, draw and illustrate in colour, sing excellently and accompany herself on the lute, and in household duties she excelled. Dear Sister Francisca had taught her well. The Convent infirmarian was adored by all the sisters. Her red, peasant face belied her heritage. She was a cousin of the great Percys of Northumberland. Her motherly heart had yearned for the bereaved child Gloucester had brought to the Convent and the Abbess left Catherine largely in her charge. She explained to the girls the King's wishes concerning her.

"He has requested that you remain here for the years of your minority and has sent gold for your welfare. We are instructed to educate you fittingly."

Over the years Catherine had heard no further mention of the King's bounty nor his interest in her future welfare.

She sat now gazing out towards the river. More and more, recently, this, the concern for her future, had worried her. She loved the Abbess and sisters dearly and her companions, the novices, but she had no wish to join them. She had other plans, though how she was to put even one into action baffled her.

She had no lands, no dower. Unless the King chose to graciously provide for her, there was naught for it but to remain among the sisterhood. Though talk of marriage was prohibited within the Convent walls, Catherine, like all girls of sixteen, had considered the possibility. Indeed — she must acquire a husband. It was a necessity, but how without dower or prospect of introduction into some noble household?

She smoothed down the grey folds of her kirtle. There were no mirrors in the house, since vanity among the sisters was not encouraged, but she knew that she was fair. Her thick ash-blonde hair hung almost straight to her waist and though she had glimpsed only distorted images of her features in the rippling waves of the river, she knew that her skin was smooth though brown from the outdoor work she shared with the sisters. Her nose appeared straight enough, small and well-shaped, though it was hard to tell under the constant changing image of the moving water. Her eyes swam out at her, large and grey, still misted as if heavy with unshed tears, but perhaps the water again gave a false impression. Sister Francisca chided her constantly about the mutinous twist of her lips.

"You've a sinful pride, child. Offer your heart to the loving Christ in true humility and your mouth will lose its pout." She'd checked her scolding at the child's wistful, bewildered air. "There, you've had much to grieve you. I tell you, child, you must learn to accept and forgive. Accept with gratitude the bounty of the King's Grace whose ward you are and forgive those who caused your sorrow. All that happens is the will of God, praise to our Blessed Saviour."

Forgive? Catherine had tried to frame the word. It would not take shape upon her lips.

Once, each year, she went to the Abbey Church to hear Requiem Mass for her father's soul. Gloucester had kept his word. Sir Wilfred Newberry's body lay in the sanctified precincts of the Abbey Church, as the Prince's remains lay under the great lantern tower in the centre of the Chancel. Poor Queen Margaret. All she held dear lay there. Only this last year had the King, having received her ransom, permitted her to sail for France. Catherine wondered if the Queen's grief and the overwhelming burden of defeat had blunted her desire for vengeance.

"I know you are high in a tree somewhere. Come down at once. The Abbess commands you."

Sister Francisca's voice. Her burly form hove into view, peering upwards uncertainly. Her unwary feet caught a partially hidden root and she stumbled. Contrite at once Catherine swung herself to the ground and ran to assist her.

Sister Francisca shook the ample folds of her habit and straightened her wimple, pulling the stiffened cloth in shape with a determined hand. She was breathing heavily. She did that more and more recently. Catherine had noted the symptom with concern.

"Nonsense," she retorted tartly when her charge had taxed her with the need to consult some physician, "do you think I do not know my own job? I'm an old woman and overheavy. I must fast more and the condition will mend."

"You bad child, you'll be the death of me. I've searched for you all over the convent when those fool girls reported you were not in the orchard."

"Sister, I am truly sorry. I wanted to be by myself. I will come."

"Let me lean on your arm a moment." The nun mopped her streaming face with a fold of her veil. "There, that's better. I'm needed to help Sister Marie Joseph in the kitchen. We have a distinguished guest."

Catherine was mystified. They did have guests, of course, but rarely noble ones, such personages being more fittingly accommodated as guests of the Abbot in the town. Who then had chosen to visit the Convent today?

"The Duchess of Gloucester is in the parlour."

Sister Francisca, having rested and recovered somewhat, steered Catherine towards the domestic buildings. "As you know she came here with Queen Margaret at the time of the battle. She was then wed to the Prince Edward, God rest his soul." Sister Francisca crossed herself devoutly. "Poor child, she has suffered much, given into the charge of His Grace of Clarence and then that terrible time in the cook shop in London." She shook her head despairingly. "I cannot think how she survived those terrifying days after her father was killed at Barnet and she so delicate and ailing."

Catherine had heard gossip concerning the Earl of Warwick's younger daughter, the Lady Anne. What fate had befallen her when she had disappeared from the Duke of Clarence's house? Some said she had herself fled from her brother-in-law who meant her ill. Certainly he had been disinclined to share the Warwick fortune with his wife's sister.

Gloucester had demanded that the lady should be found at once. There had been scenes, they said, in Westminster Palace when the angry brothers had confronted the King. It was Gloucester who found her in the end and conveyed her to the Sanctuary of St. Martin le Grand, then, in the following year, she had become his bride and gone with him to her father's former castle of Middleham.

Some pitied the little Duchess, fearing that the stern and ruthless Duke, her husband, would not keep her long, that his only desire for her hand had been heightened by the amount of her fortune and that she would die prematurely in mysterious circumstances. Others countered the accusation hotly. The Duke had ever held affection for his cousin since his own days at Middleham in the Earl of Warwick's service. His true affection, they said, had saved her from a scullion's life in the cook shop of London's Chepeside and his care had restored her health. Had she not given him a son?

So the Duchess was here in the Abbess's parlour.

Catherine had an overwhelming desire to look on the face of Gloucester's wife. She only half-heard the rest of Sister Francisca's diatribe.

"She has brought us a gift, fifty golden nobles for the restoration of the Lady Chapel. The Duke is in the town viewing the Lantern Tower in the Abbey. His Grace the King, it seems, has given instructions for improvements to the Abbey Church."

Catherine looked down hurriedly at her crumpled kirtle. "I must change this and put on a clean coif and wimple in case I am sent to help serve in the parlour."

Sister Francisca nodded and Catherine dashed into the stone-flagged corridor to be met with reproving glances from the Mistress of the Novices. She slowed down to a walk, hastened to the dortour to put to rights her appearance, then went to the kitchens to offer assistance.

The Abbess did send for her. Sister Marie Joseph impatiently bade her remove her apron and go at once to the parlour.

Catherine paused in the doorway and curtsied low.

A pleasant low voice bade her rise and she came in and hesitantly waited for the Abbess to present her. Under lowered lids she regarded the Duchess intently.

She was no beauty but others would always remember her as one. Perhaps it was her air of extreme fragility. She was wearing a kirtle of green silk, girdled in gold, with the new truncated butterfly hennin over a matching gold cap embroidered with seed pearls. Only the faintest wisps of her bright gold Neville hair showed beneath her veil. Her face was rather too long for beauty, the cheek bones standing out gauntly, though today they were flushed with colour. It was the gentleness of expression which gave loveliness to the features and the unusual blue, almost violet eyes. The mouth drooped becomingly, but Catherine was later to learn it was no mark of petulance or lack of strength of will. The little Duchess could bring a wealth of determination to her assistance when needed. If she had indeed been married against her will and was dominated by her husband, she showed no such marks of suffering. She appeared supremely happy and in the full flush of her womanhood. Catherine could not take her eyes from the quality of the silk or its bright splash of emerald colour against the white-washed walls of the parlour and the more subdued hues of the nun's black habit and her own dove-grey gown.

The Abbess addressed the Duchess respectfully.

"This is the girl, Your Grace. She has been with us now full six years."

Anne of Gloucester put out a hand in welcome. "I hear you are a ward of the Crown, mistress, and came here with My Lord of Gloucester."

Catherine bowed her head. "He brought me here after —" she hesitated — "after the battle. My father was among those Lancastrian knights executed by order of the Lord Constable of England."

The Duchess's violet-blue eyes clouded with pity. "I understand your grief. I too had my sorrows after that bloody battle and indeed before that at Barnet." She gave a little sigh, turning to an older lady who waited behind her chair. "I pray those wars are now over and that Edward has given lasting peace to England. My Richard works day and night to keep the North safe for the King. The border is rarely quiet but we are secure at Middleham, praise God."

Her attendant nodded agreement. The Duchess turned again to Catherine.

"Were your estates confiscated or does the King hold the land in trust for you?"

"I understand the King granted my father's manor to our cousin, Sir Hugh Kingsford. There were no male heirs and the land is entailed."

The Duchess frowned. "Then the King provides for you?" She regarded the demurely-clad girl with pity. She had not forgotten the time when her father had been declared rebel and her inheritance was in dispute. She thrust aside the unpleasant memories of those dark days in the Clarence household when even Isobel had seemed her enemy, her young husband slain and the rumours said by Gloucester's hand. Now her future was secure and her son, her darling Edward, safe, waiting for her return in his nurse's care at Middleham. At least her father and uncle the Marquess of Montecute had been spared the final ignominy of the headsman's axe. Both had fallen at Barnet. This girl had had to face that unendurable sorrow.

"The King has been graciously generous. We have received gold in plenty for the care of Mistress Newberry." The Abbess was anxious to assure the King's sister-in-law she had no complaint.

She excused herself as a timid knock came at the door and a frightened novice whispered hastily that she was needed in the infirmary. The Duchess was quick to assure her that she would feel no neglect if the Abbess went about her duties.

"I know you are always busied about the affairs of this house, Reverend Mother. Mary is anxious to see the Convent quarters. May she go with you? I will be happy in the company of Mistress Newberry."

The two women curtsied and left. Anne of Gloucester pointed to a joint stool near her chair.

"Will you not sit, mistress? What is your given name?"

Catherine obeyed clumsily. She had expected the Duchess to be quite unlike this friendly, capable woman. "Catherine," she said in a whisper.

"What will you do, Catherine? Will you take the veil?"

"No." The answer was immediate and Anne smiled.

"You feel no vocation?"

"No, Your Grace."

"Have you petitioned the King to allow you to leave the Convent?"

"No, Your Grace. How can I? I have nowhere to go."

"It is time they found a husband for you."

Catherine flushed hotly and Anne leaned

forward to catch her expression.

"Do you fear a forced match?"

Catherine lifted her grey eyes to the Duchess's blue ones. "I think not. I cannot expect freedom of choice. I know nothing of the world outside the Convent. I was but a child when I came here but the nuns have taught me well. I would not have you think I have been neglected here."

"But you are now sixteen."

"I have no dower, Your Grace. It will not be easy to provide me with a husband. It may be that I must take the veil."

"Against your will? No, that would be unwise. The King is not so cruel." She gave a little merry laugh. "He is no saint, our Edward. He will understand your natural desire for a home of your own and children."

"But my father was judged traitor —" Catherine broke off uncertainly.

"That is so, but for that you cannot be held responsible." Anne considered. "I think it good for you to enter some noble household. Would you not wish to serve as lady-in-waiting, at least for a time until you are re-established in the world again?"

Catherine's grey eyes gleamed but as swiftly she veiled them with her dark lashes.

"That has ever been my hope, Your Grace —"

"Leave this to me, Catherine. I will take up your cause. You remind me of myself at your age. I will see to it that My Lord of Gloucester writes immediately to the King. Your future will be assured, I promise, and I will not permit you to be given into some shameful match. Will you trust me?"

Impulsively Catherine kissed the little white hand, laid light on the Duchess's chair arm.

Both women looked up startled as the door was thrust open, expecting to see the Abbess and the Lady Mary returned so soon from their errand. They were both surprised to see Richard of Gloucester in the doorway.

Anne held out her arms in greeting. "Dickon, finished so soon?"

His grey-green eyes passed from his wife's flushed face to the lowered head of the girl who rose and curtsied low. He walked behind the Duchess's chair and placed his hands affectionately upon her shoulders.

"This is Mistress Catherine Newberry, My Lord. You will perhaps remember that you brought her to this house after the battle."

"Indeed, I do remember." His voice was musical. She had not thought it so. "Will you not sit down again, mistress." He waved her courteously to the stool. She looked up to find his eyes glinting as if with some memory which had amused him. That mouth, which

she had remembered as hard and tightly held in, was relaxed and the corners twitched with mirth. He seemed smaller, then she recalled in the Abbey he had been dwarfed by his brothers. During these years she had thought of him as huge, a stern, implacable judge, without understanding or mercy. Now she was strangely at a loss in his presence.

"Did you not say you preferred life as a beggar to the protection the Convent offered? Or was it my assistance you rejected?"

She coloured hotly. "Your Grace will recall that I was over young, and spoke under stress of grief."

The laughter left his eyes and he nodded gravely.

"I have not forgotten. I but tease you, mistress, since it seems you have bloomed under the care of the nuns."

"Yet Mistress Newberry is now anxious to leave the Convent, Dickon." Anne of Gloucester's voice was eager. "I had thought you might do her the kindness of petitioning the King that she might enter some household, my own, if it pleases you."

He eyed Catherine again with that hint of mockery.

"If it is what Mistress Newberry wishes. Perhaps she would prefer to serve in some less markedly Yorkist household since her sympathies are so clearly Lancastrian."

Catherine felt hot colour again flood her face and throat. She did not look at him.

"I assure Your Grace I would be grateful for any assistance you could offer. If, in the past, I have been grossly impertinent, I beg your forgiveness. I am in no position to ask where I might serve. I know well I rely on the good offices of those who will succour me."

She waited in an agony for him to make some reply heavy with irony. He did not do so and she expelled her breath in a little sigh of relief.

"If Your Grace would excuse me —" She rose and faced them respectfully.

Anne of Gloucester held out her hand for the girl to kiss. "Be of good courage. My Lord will help you." She turned to him for confirmation. "Is it not so, Dickon?"

The intimate use of the family name seemed at odds with all Catherine had heard of him.

He raised one eyebrow sardonically.

"I have said I will do as you wish." He waved Catherine to the door and moved to seat himself on the joint stool near his wife.

"You may go, mistress. God guard you."

She curtsied low and withdrew.

Outside in the corridor she encountered Joan, her eyelids puffy as if she had recently been weeping bitterly.

"Joan, what is it?"

"Sister Francisca has collapsed. She was gasping for breath when she returned to the infirmary. She seemed so ill that the Abbess was sent for. She has summoned a physician from the town. We are exhorted to pray for her. Oh, Catherine, what shall we do if she is taken from us?"

The girl hurried off and Catherine stood stock-still in the shaded chill of the stone-flagged corridor. The sun did not reach her and she felt a thrill of fear. Not since that terrible day in the market square had it touched her so. Now, as then, she had to stiffen her knees and subdue the sudden weakness of her belly. Someone she loved dearly was in peril. She must be strong. She would be needed. Anxiety must not be allowed to cloud her judgement, making her inefficient in her office. She crossed herself, said a muttered prayer to the Virgin and a second to her patron saint, Catherine, and went with a firm tread towards the infirmary.

CHAPTER II

Sister Francisca died during the third night following her attack. She had been nursed devotedly by her fellow sisters, and when they were not by her side prayers were offered for her constantly in the Chapel. Catherine seldom left her where she lay in the hard little bed in the spotlessly scrubbed, bare cell of the Convent infirmary. The physician had been dubious from the start. Her heart was impaired, he had said, some disease. He believed she had bravely concealed many attacks of severe pain. There was little he could do. He gave instructions for the preparation of pain-relieving herbal compounds, came each day, but it was obvious to Catherine's eyes, made keen as they were by anxiety and devotion, that the burly nun grew weaker each day.

She was barely conscious and her breathing became stertorous, her lips paling to purplish blue. Catherine tended her, bathing the roughened skin of her forehead and throat, where they'd loosened her wimple and for the first time Catherine saw how fine and white her skin was where the sun and the wind of the outdoor work of the Convent had not taken its toll.

Her relatives were informed but it would be weeks before the letter, carried slowly by carrier's cart, could be answered and it became clear to the Abbess that her loved infirmarian would be cold clay and laid reverently in the burial ground of the Convent long before any reply could be expected.

Sister Francisca received the last rites from the Convent chaplain on the evening of March 28th, 1477, and died quietly later during the night. She was not able to speak coherently to her loved charge, and when Catherine forsook the pathetic cell to pray with the sisters in the Chapel, she was, in some strange way, glad that it should be so. Had Sister Francisca demanded of her any oath of forgiveness for those who had dealt her such terrible blows, she could not have withheld it, loving the nun as she did. But it could not be. Men had caused the death of her father while other — more guilty men — had escaped the consequences of their actions on Tewkesbury field. They would pay for it — all of them, Edward the King, who had commanded his indictment, George of Clarence, who had singled him out as doubly heinous traitor there in the Abbey, and

Richard of Gloucester who had condemned him and seen him die. There was one other Catherine judged in her own heart as not free of guilt for her father's spilt blood. Hugh Kingsford had received the gift of his land. Had he too sworn false evidence against him? She could not be sure but she would discover the truth for herself. If Kingsford was guilty, then somehow, cost what it would, he would pay with the others. Six years ago she had sworn it, here in this same Chapel where, doubtless, Margaret of Anjou had knelt and prayed for victory and the safety of her son. Now, here again, she renewed her vow.

Though all understood her particular grief and strove to comfort her, the Convent precincts seemed to imprison her after Sister Francisca had gone. She strove to conquer her restless spirit, gave extra attention to her embroidery and music, spent long hours weeding and hoeing in the herb garden and vegetable gardens, as if energetic, exhausting activity would tire her out so completely that she would sleep without dreams in her hard, clean little bed in the Convent dortour, but sleep evaded her nightly and when she did slide off at last into exhausted oblivion her enemies loomed immense in her troubled dreams, the three Royal Brothers, their armour dented, gleaming and dappled with blood, menaced her with drawn swords and battle-axes upheld. Once she woke screaming, alarming her companions, as again the headsman's axe was lifted from the straw, its edge red dyed from the sun's rays, and hovered above her threateningly.

No news came from the court. The Abbess did not reprove her when she neglected her duties sometimes, her eyes far away, hands idle in her lap. Now, more than ever since she had seen Gloucester again, she must leave this place. If before she had received no guidance from her prayers for vengeance, in what way she might bring about her one fixed intent, now she glimpsed only dimly, yet still it was there to linger and grow in her mind, one way she might deal the first of her enemies a mortal blow.

Gloucester loved his wife. Catherine had known it instantly. Say what they might, Richard of Gloucester adored his ailing Duchess and she worshipped him. Their eyes had only to meet for those in their presence to know the truth. If he had married her in the first instance to acquire his share of her inheritance, he had learned to love her.

It was clear that she was also delicate. In time heaven itself would deal Richard of Gloucester repayment in kind for any grief he had afforded the widows and orphans and those who had died on Tewkesbury field. Anne would weaken and die prematurely. The signs were there and both knew it — but for the present they dwelt secure in the love they gave to each other. If the Duchess's trust in her husband could be broken, then Catherine would have her revenge.

Richard was but a man, young, virile, and if Catherine was any judge, passionate. There must be times when his wife's weakness caused frustrated desire to tear his loins. He could be tempted. He could fall from grace and his wife's anguish wound him sorely. Catherine considered the possibilities. She was likely not to his taste but there would be other women. If she could insinuate herself into the good graces of the Duchess, and she had made a fair beginning, even if she were not of the Gloucester household itself, she could begin to poison Gloucester's peace. For the moment she must force herself to wait in patience.

By the middle of May the weather had become unexpectedly hot. Sister Boniface had succeeded Sister Francisca as infirmarian and Catherine was requested to assist her in compounding ointments and draughts in the stillroom. The new infirmarian was a young nun, efficient when not harassed, which she frequently was. She spent all her days flying from pallet to pallet, from there to kitchens and stillroom, her wimple awry and her keys constantly ajingle at her waist.

Catherine worked steadily with her pestle and mortar, her kirtle girdled to her waist, her sleeves pushed high and though she had achieved the trick of remaining as still as humanly possible in these trying days, the sweat was heavy on her brow and she felt the unpleasant trickle from her armpits. She smiled wryly as Sister Boniface charged in, scarlet in the face, gleaming with sweat and out of breath as usual.

"That stupid girl," she said crossly, "left the milk out in the sun. There'll not be a spot we can offer the three sick sisters tonight."

"It's possible they'll prefer ale, sister. It's more cooling."

"Think you so? Milk is better for them." She pushed back her wimple wearily easing her fingers beneath her chin.

"Well," she demanded, flustered, as a novice thrust her head round the door.

"I'm sorry, sister. The Abbess commands Mistress Catherine's presence in the parlour. At once."

Catherine made an exclamation of dismay. She was in no state to go to the Abbess. She tore off her coarse apron and the cord which held her kirtle high, smoothed its folds and snatched up napkin to mop her sweating brow and wipe clammy fingers.

"You look well enough," Sister Boniface nodded approval. "Hurry, Catherine, she must want you urgently."

Rising from her respectful curtsy Catherine almost stumbled in her agitation. The sun streamed from the opened casement behind the seated Abbess full on to the face of her visitor. Richard of Gloucester looked elegant, despite the heat, in a doublet of murrey velvet, a chain of linked enamelled York roses and suns relieving its sober hue.

"My Lord," Catherine stammered hastily.

"I brought you here. See, I come to take you away." He raised his shoulders and let them fall in a little gesture of sardonic amusement.

"Take me away? Reverend Mother, why, where?" Catherine was confused. The news she eagerly awaited came so soon.

"My child, we shall regret losing you, but the Duke is pleased to place you in his household to serve the Duchess and I cannot but think this will be an excellent opportunity for you." She rose and took Catherine's trembling hand. "My Lord Duke, will you give her time to bid goodbye to the sisters, if I go and summon them together in the refectory?"

Catherine was suddenly terrified. She groped for words — "I am to go, today, this moment, without days to prepare?"

"I am afraid it must be today. I ride north to Middleham. It is convenient if you go in my train." As usual with him he became understanding after his mood of light raillery. "There is time." He indicated a basket of woven rushes on the floor near the Abbess's table. "I have brought you more suitable garments. Will you go and change and take your leave of the sisters. By your courtesy, Reverend Mother, I will take refreshment in your parlour."

The Abbess inclined her head, curtsied and made to withdraw. "I will send refreshment, Your Grace," she said quietly. "Catherine, come."

In the dortour Catherine tore at the basket's fastenings with impatient fingers. At last it was done and she reached in apprehensively in case her vain desire would be met with disappointment. It was not so. The gown of dark blue silk shimmered in the sun from the high window and there was a kirtle of fine white linen and a wide girdle trimmed with seed pearls. She tore off her grey kirtle of wolsey linsey and drew the shimmering thing over her head.

When Joan entered some moments later

Catherine was fingering worriedly the expanse of bare throat and shoulder and the neck was cut so low her young firm breasts were revealed, thrusting upwards to show dark rosebud teats under the braided decoration of the neckline.

"Joan, I cannot wear this," she said, horrified.

The novice laughed and crossed to her side.

"Foolish one, there is a little vest here, see, trimmed with gold braid and pearls. Oh, Catherine, how lovely." She smoothed the silk with work-roughened hands and, as quickly, crossed herself.

"I must not be envious. Such vain dress is not for me, but I rejoice for you. Let me fit the hennin. Push back your hair so. Sister Boniface says when she left the Court four years ago the Queen had instituted a new fashion of shaving the front hair back, yes, and all hair from the brows too." She frowned. "It would be a pity to hide your beautiful hair."

She turned away and Catherine hugged her close. "Joan, you are weeping. Do you regret your decision? You have not taken final vows. If you speak to Reverend Mother —"

The novice shook back her tears. "No, it is not so. I regret nothing. My father had no wish to place me here. I was not coerced. I am determined to give my life to God. It is what I want. Now and again I have doubts. It is natural. Sister Francisca said she scourged herself again and again when she thought of the feasts and the dancing, she was at Court you know, and the jousts and the hunting." Joan's lip trembled. "Dear Sister Francisca, we loved her so. And now you are to leave us. Nothing will be the same again. The Virgin guard you, Catherine."

Catherine drew back as the little novice opened the door.

"Are you afraid?"

Catherine nodded. "Yes, oh yes, Joan, I am afraid."

"But you are so fortunate. Did you hope to go to London instead of the North? Is this a disappointment? Is that it?"

Catherine's alarm changed to joy. "No, of course it is not. I have seen the Duchess of Gloucester. She is gentle and young. I shall take pleasure in serving her. I have no ambition to go to Court." She caught back the final word "yet" she had meant to utter.

"Then we must not keep his Grace of Gloucester waiting. The sisters are gathered in the refectory to bid you goodbye."

Afterwards Catherine was thankful that respect for the Duke made them cut short her goodbyes. Her ties were broken swiftly and painlessly. To have lingered would have half broken her heart. Each kissed her tenderly without words and the Abbess pressed into her hands a little velvet covered box and a Book of Hours, bound in white silk and embroidered in gold thread.

"Do not forget us," she chided gently. "The carrier's cart brings us letters though slowly. I shall look to hear from you of your new life and of the health of the little Duchess. So do not fail us."

Catherine bowed her head for the final blessing and tremulously prepared to re-enter the parlour.

She waited anxiously for some comment on her appearance from her new master. He smiled as he rose, pushing aside the ale cup and platter which the Abbess had provided on his request.

"I see I chose well."

She stared at him wonderingly. "You chose, My Lord?"

"Certainly. Have I not ridden from London? I break my journey to collect the person of my new ward." He moved towards her, noting her mounting alarm. "You *are* my ward. His Grace the King has exhorted me to find you a suitable husband. That might be difficult. My rough spoken, hard riding men of the North may not be to your taste."

"Nor I to theirs, Your Grace."

He grinned his acceptance of her only veiled insolence.

"That is better. I had memories of a child of spirit I carried here. I feared the nuns might have destroyed it utterly in making such an obedient, respectful lady of you."

Her hand moved agitatedly to her heart, still aware of the revealing cut of her new gown, its inadequacies not entirely dealt with by the modesty vest of gold brocaded velvet. She was close to tears. For some reason this man had the power to both repel and attract. One moment he treated her as a child, goading her to near rudeness, the next with studied gentleness.

"My Lord Duke, I had no wish to be pert. Believe me I am truly grateful."

The courtesy she found wholly winning returned immediately. He took her trembling little hand and kissed it with such gravity she could not believe he still teased her.

"I know it, Mistress Catherine. Now let us go for we have a long ride ahead. Did you pack your belongings in the basket?"

"It is at the door, Your Grace."

He led her out to the main gate of the Convent. The portress had unbarred it, her face averted to hide her tears at parting. Catherine turned once. The familiar warm, red brick swam in a haze of blurred vision with the orchard, the Chapel and the distant view of one bend of the river.

A litter was drawn up in readiness. Catherine hesitated and the Duke urged her forward.

"I have never travelled so, My Lord," she said hesitantly. "Before, I always rode with my father."

"Indeed?" he said arching one brow upwards. "But how long since you rode hard and fast? No, mistress, today you will ride as I bid you. Later we will see."

She climbed clumsily within while the Duke's men in their Yorkist livery of murrey and blue strapped the basket containing her few belongings on to one of the sumpters. The Duke mounted. Catherine leaned forward as they clattered over the cobbles of the town past the North door of the Abbey then through the market square with its poignant memories. It was bare and empty of people. This hot afternoon they would seek the shade of their shops or the leafy trees in the small gardens. No scaffold dominated its centre. Catherine saw the sunlight light up the pennons with the emblazoned White Boar of Gloucester. Was it her imagination that they were tinged with a faint blood red light or was it still too early for the reddish glow of the sinking sun to yet light the sky? She sank back in the litter. Indeed, she must have been mistaken.

CHAPTER III

The heat had lessened when they reached the Yorkshire Dales. It had been insupportable in York. The stinks from the kennels and the town's shambles had all but nauseated Catherine. Only in the Minster where the Duke had ordered requiems for the souls of his father and brother, Edmund of Rutland, slain after Wakefield, was there any relief from the squalor of the town streets. Among the soaring, sandstone pillars of the aisle it was possible to breathe easily and appreciate the sweet scent of incense from the High Altar and the soothing chant of plain-song. Today the Duke lit a candle for the soul of the latest member of his family who had died. Isobel of Clarence, his wife's elder sister and wife of his brother, George, had died in childbed on December 24th of 1476. She had ever ailed and it was rumoured even at Tewkesbury that the Duke's rule of her had been harsh. Now she was laid to rest and the babe with her in the family vault in Tewkesbury Abbey.

Catherine had wondered, during the journey, if she would come into contact with the elder of the Yorkist Princes. Gloucester had stayed at Warwick Castle to visit his nephew, young Edward and niece, the Lady Margaret. The Duke was not in residence. Catherine was half disappointed, half relieved. From then their journey north continued, a weary, irritating business. The heat, dust and flies intensifying all their discomfort; through Coventry, Leicester, Nottingham, Newark on the Trent, then on to York, and now, at last, praise the sweet Virgin, the fresh air of the North gave welcome relief.

At last the Duke gave consent for Catherine to ride and a palfrey was provided for her. She rejoiced in the release from the stifling sickening swaying of the litter and did not take long to regain her own skilful control of her mount. She rode in the centre of the procession, ahead and behind her Gloucester's men-at-arms in their leathern jacks and salets, bearing his device of the White Boar. He rode near the van. She could see his black destrier now picking its way delicately. To the rear, more slowly, came the sumpters loaded with armour and equipment, one or two waggons and supply carts. An elderly maid Gloucester had acquired for her in Coventry jogged along slightly behind, riding pillion, her arms clutching fearfully at the waist of one of the Duke's squires.

Gloucester halted his mount and sidled to the roadside, signalling for Catherine to ride forward.

"You ride well after so long a time."

"My father taught me. I hunted with him and had a peregrine of my own." In her eagerness to speak of her former delight in the outdoor sport of the countryside, she forget that she had again tactlessly spoken of the bone of contention between them. He appeared not to notice but continued to point out to her places of interest on their way.

"We shall soon see the battlements of Middleham. We shall be home before the evening. I had thought you might delay me and we might be a day or even two days longer."

"I am no weakling, Your Grace, though convent bred."

He chuckled. "Aye, I know, but the heat is debilitating. You stood the confinement of the litter well. I feared the onset of sickness. Anne is often embarrassed so."

She lowered her grey eyes. As always his lips curved in relaxation and those stern eyes lighted up whenever he mentioned Anne's name. Catherine doubted if, even in London, he had consoled himself in her absence. Yet he had two acknowledged bastards, they said, a boy, John, and a younger daughter, named like herself, Catherine.

Now the hills had given way to meadowland, pasture for sheep, bordered by trees and hedgerows and at last Middleham itself clustering round the massive strength of the castle.

They clattered over the drawbridge and under the gatehouse. Already grooms and servants gathered in the inner ward since for an hour their progress must have been noted by the eagle-eyed guardians on the battlements, as they saw the glint of sun on the cold metal of lance and pikes and at last the pennons of Gloucester as the procession wound its way towards the little market town.

At the head of the keep stair stood Anne of Gloucester in a gown of brown and gold brocade and a tall, steeple hennin of cloth of gold and gauze veiling. Gloucester dismounted and mounted the stairs at a run. As Catherine was assisted to alight by a youthful page she looked up at the two near the keep entrance. She heard the Duchess laugh but could catch nothing of what was said. Then, at last, he remembered her and summoned her to approach.

Anne held out her hand in greeting.

"Welcome to Middleham, Catherine. I shall call you that now, since you are to attend me. We want you to be happy here."

Catherine kissed the Duchess's slim fingers.

"Your Grace, I know that I shall be."

"Don't become too attached," the Duke was teasing again, "or I shall never marry you off. Remember your marriage must bring me some advantage or I wasted my time at Gupshill on both occasions."

Anne shot him a glance of reproof. "Heed not his quips, Catherine, I have sworn that I shall not allow them to sell you. Now come with me. I will present you to my other attendants and to my mother, the Countess of Warwick."

The Great Keep of Middleham had been renovated and Catherine marvelled as she entered the Great Hall on the first floor. It seemed large enough to engulf the whole of the Convent buildings. She peered upwards at the gabled wooden roof then down the length of the hall to the open hearth in the centre, now unused. A woman sat in a high carved seat by one of the windows, her head bent over some embroidery to catch the best of the light.

She turned at their entry and Catherine thought she caught resemblances to the Duchess in her long thin face with its high cheekbones and acquiline nose. She was sombrely dressed in a gown of dark grey velvet, though Catherine thought the day over-warm for such material. She was unattended and her expression, as she rose to greet them, was wistful, faintly withdrawn, as though life had passed her by. This then was the Duchess's mother, the dowager Countess of Warwick, widow of the dread Kingmaker. She greeted Gloucester with warmth, her gaunt cheeks flushing with faint colour.

"You are earlier than we hoped, Richard. I thought Anne's eagerness misplaced when the word came from the Gatehouse Watch, but I see I was mistaken and I am glad of it. Welcome home, My Lord."

He flung himself down on a chair near her and called for ale. A minute page, black hair oddly cut and standing up on end as if someone had seized it and attempted to scalp him, scrambled immediately down the stairs to the kitchens below. Anne sat beside her mother and drew Catherine to her side.

"This is Catherine Newberry, mother. You remember we discussed the possibility of her joining the household."

Catherine found herself flush under the Countess's sharp eyes. The Duchess pressed her gently to a stool near her feet.

"Can you sew well, child?" the Countess shot at her.

Catherine nodded, then, meeting the Duke's quizzical glance, said, "Indeed I think I will satisfy you, madam. The nuns taught me strictly." She felt that the Countess had interest in few members of the household and it would be harder to please her than her young mistress. Since she was not yet dismissed and had no notion of where to retire, she sat quietly while family matters were discussed.

"How is the King's Grace, Dickon? Is the Queen well? Tell us of the Court."

Anne reached for her mother's stitchery to trace her fingers appreciatively round the design.

"I have already satisfied him about Ned's health. I sent the nurse to fetch him. He seemed tired this afternoon and I insisted he should sleep. The heat has irritated him."

The Duke nodded, lazily content, as the page raced back to his chair with the ale cup. He thanked the lad and, as he moved to withdraw, pulled him sharply back, turning his face to the light. Catherine saw that the boy's right eye was ringed with a faint tracing of yellowy mauve bruising.

"I see you bit the dust. Clumsiness?"

The boy eyed him respectfully. "I fell in the tilt yard."

"Not assisted by hand or boot, I trust?"

The lad's head shook emphatically. "No, sir. It was my fault, truly."

Gloucester rumpled his untidy mop of dark

hair and waved him away. He smiled at Anne's unspoken question.

"I'll not have the child bullied. He's over-young. I've not forgotten my own days of paging and squiring. I was undersized and came in for no little contempt and teasing. Mind you, I'll not have the lads shirk either."

Catherine gazed briefly at his right shoulder. It was rumoured that it was perceptibly higher than his left, but she had not noted any mark of deformity in the journey north. She had heard it whispered that the Duke, Cecily of York's youngest surviving child, had been ill-formed since birth and crippled. "Crouch-back" was his nickname, levelled at him behind his back. "Crook backed Dick."

She wondered at the wealth of scorn the child might have had to face. The loneliness of State would cause the youthful prince to stand apart from his fellows. This then had caused him to hold affinity for what must be the most youthful member of his household.

He was imparting family news, his thirst satisfied.

"Ned is well, though he overeats and takes not enough exercise. I charged him with it but he merely laughs. He takes it well from me. The Queen is elegant as ever." He was reticent on that subject and Catherine noticed the tightening of lips the Countess made when Elizabeth Woodville was mentioned. She seemed not popular with the Countess or her son-in-law. "The children thrive. Edward's Ned goes soon to Ludlow under River's tutorlege. He does well, they say. Little Dickon is a squirming, affectionate monkey, like this one of our own."

He stood up and waited, arms outstretched, as a child pattered up the stairs and ran forward, his head butting his father's waist. The nurse came panting up behind. "Lord Edward, you have no cause to greet your father so. 'Tis time you were more respectful." As Richard lifted the boy high into the air, while his mother and grandam laughed, she tutted her displeasure. "It's true what I say. He's five years grown. Soon he must leave your care to be page. He'll not then be so spoilt."

"Peace, Nan," the Duke laughed. "Well, Ned, have you been a good lad to your mother and grandam?"

"And to nurse? That's more to the point," the woman sniffed, her pertness allowable from long service in a familiar and loved household.

"And to your nurse?"

"Yes, My lord father, truly. I have been having my riding lessons. Jehan says I can have my pony soon. Lord father, you will order it so?"

The child's tone was wheedling and Catherine was touched, despite herself, at sight of them together. He was a beautiful child though delicate like his mother. He had inherited the Neville fairness and his skin was soft, almost transparent like a girl's. Catherine looked at the slight limbs. Would he ever bear the weight of armour and have the strength to wield axe or battle sword? For his age he seemed so small-boned and light of weight. His brain was active enough. He prattled away in his light, high voice and he seemed well served for half the household's names were on his lips as friends and attendants.

Gloucester, at length, set him down and ordered the nurse to remove him to the nursery.

"Rest now and you shall eat with us tonight in the small chamber."

"My Lord!" The nurse's shocked tones were arrested by an authoritative note in the Duke's answer, gentle but pointed enough.

"I have spoken, Nan. He'll take no harm if he rests now and I have seen little of him of late. The sooner he becomes used to dining in company the better."

The boy leaned forward impulsively for a final hug and was regretfully withdrawn by his nurse to his mother's gentle admonition to be obedient.

She turned worriedly to Richard.

"Nan is right, Dickon. He is becoming spoilt. We must take care but he ails so often —" She broke off and he leaned across to pat her hand.

"Not so much lately. I am pleased to see him so lively." He frowned. "George's Ned seems backward still, though Margaret is pretty and happy enough."

"Did you see Clarence?" The Countess's question was sharp. Did Catherine detect a further note of asperity. Had she ever forgiven her other son-in-law his betrayal of her husband before Barnet?

"No." Gloucester's reply was equally abrupt. There was bad blood between them since the affair of the Duke's wooing of Anne and the disposal of her inheritance.

Anne said diffidently, "Both George and the children must feel the loss of Isobel."

The Countess gave a snort of derision and caught a sudden glint in the Duke's eyes.

"She saw little of them for them to heed her absence, poor bairns. As for George's treatment of Isobel, the least said soonest mended."

Gloucester looked pointedly at Catherine. "I think Mistress Newberry must be wearied."

Anne rose and called the page forward.

"Will, take Mistress Newberry to her apartment in the South wall. She is to share with Marian and Bridget. See to the disposal of her baggage." She smiled at Catherine. "We have neglected you, but I think you will find the other girls friendly. They are both daughters of local barons. Marian is slightly older than you and soon to be wed. Bridget is younger. They will take charge of you and show you to your place here in the Great Hall for supper. We shall eat tonight in the privy chamber."

Catherine curtsied and followed the page down the winding stairs, across the grassy court at the rear of the Keep to the South Curtain Wall. Here he guided her up the stairs to a small sleeping chamber and rushed off to arrange for her belongings to be delivered.

It was a small room but luxurious enough to Catherine used to the sharing of a small dortour with the novices and the stern mistress who presided over their care.

Two girls sat perched on one of the truckle beds examining the broken clasp of a pretty enamelled pendant.

The older girl spoke to Catherine, hesitant in the doorway.

"You must be Catherine Newberry. The Duchess says you are to take my place when I leave next week to be wed."

Catherine nodded, shyly.

"Well come in." She pointed. "It will be crowded until I leave. You are to sleep there near the wall. This is Bridget Ransom. She is niece to Lord Scrope."

The younger, fairer girl giggled faintly and the older girl, obviously The Lady Marian said, "You will be hard put to keep her in order. Stop laughing, Bridget. The Countess says the sooner some man takes you to wife and a switch to your back the better. Even then I fear he'll have a hard bargain."

Bridget made no answer but Catherine thought the future husband would find no cause for complaint. She was as pretty as a picture, with a round childish face and merry brown eyes. Marian might be more stately and a good chatelaine for her husband's household but she lacked the charm of her gay companion. Nevertheless she made Catherine welcome and at length she warmed to the dark, sallow-featured girl's capable handling of her instalment into the household and her amazing practicality. Catherine would find it a hard task to replace her adequately in the Duchess's service.

She settled more quickly into the household at Middleham than she would have believed possible. The work was not arduous, in fact Catherine secretly began to long for more exhausting tasks to keep her occupied, since the

Duchess was completely undemanding. Marian Preston left Middleham one week after Catherine's arrival to marry her young baron. She went laden with gifts from the Gloucesters, the Duchess's gentle admonitions and good wishes ringing in her ears. Her father, a burly, quiet-spoken man, received her with pleasure, for she had made her mark at Middleham and Sir William craved Gloucester's favour as did all the Northern knights. Since Bridget was indeed sadly impractical Catherine immediately assumed Marian Preston's duties, attending the Duchess when she rode out, assisting her in her embroidery, running errands, but there were many hours of the day when Anne graciously dismissed her to seek entertainment for herself.

The family dined often in private so she saw little of Gloucester though when the local nobles flocked to the Castle the Duke entertained them royally in the Great Hall and Catherine saw for the first time he was indeed uncrowned King of the North. Her soul, starved for so long of the luxuries and fripperies delighted in during girlhood, thrilled to the splendour of the feasting when the lighted brands lit up the bosses of the splendid roof, glinting on the golden collars of the lords and the necklaces and pendants of their ladies.

The rich foods, variety of courses and subleties were too much for her, used as she was to the more simple fare at Gupshill. She toyed with the venison, roast meat, fowls in their spiced sauces and rejected the horrifying delicacies of peacock and larks tongues. Such creatures pleased her in their living states and she thought she would not easily become accustomed to dismissing them simply as table fare.

She had been concerned about her lack of suitable attire but the Duchess informed her, gaily, that the King had requested that they equip her as befitted her station.

"You are to have a settlement on your betrothal and until then a generous allowance. You must not fear that you are accepting charity. Such is not the case. It is the King's duty and his goodwill to provide for you."

Catherine wondered secretly if this indeed were so, and whether the Duchess generously exceeded that amount, for silks and brocades, jewels and hennins were ordered from York and the Castle needlewomen hastened to complete hurriedly the gowns and fine shifts for Catherine's sadly depleted wardrobe. Bridget was entranced and spent hours advising and admiring.

The child was a friendly companion but her talk was indeed of naught but romance and Courts of love and Catherine found it difficult sometimes to hold back a sharp retort. She was thankful her bedmate was no scornful, noble daughter of some great house. To the Duchess Bridget was of no use at all. When needed she was never at hand. She was constantly near the tiltyard watching the young squires at their practice with the quintain. During feasts she danced until exhausted and was often sick for days following, through over-indulgence in the sweetmeats. Catherine was afraid she would be fat and near enough toothless before she was thirty, but for all her idle self-indulgence she was generous to a fault and her gossip extremely illuminating. One of her latest admirers had gone with Gloucester in the King's train to France, in 1475 and Catherine discovered much about the Duke's character from Bridget's chatter of the feasts and Councils and the dearth of fighting.

"Phillip says the Duke returned disgusted. He would never have accepted the French King's bribes but would have fought it out there and then while the English nobles and merchants had been persuaded to pay the costs of the expedition. Philip says our Dickon's a second Harry the Fifth in battle. He's been with the Duke on border forays and into Scotland."

"Surely it is fairer to make peace," Catherine said practically, "for the good of the realm. Wars cost money which must be extorted from the poor."

Bridget shrugged expressively. It was clear she had never seen a battle, nor the defeated wounded huddling beneath the walls of the Abbey nave. It would have been useless to attempt to make her understand. To Bridget war meant the excitement and colour of the tourney and she regretted that such entertainment was rarely staged at Middleham.

One other side of Gloucester Catherine was to see, Gloucester the auditor and man of business. His clerks were constantly engaged on lawsuits, tallies and accounts and each day the Duke summoned them to his chamber. Anne would sigh.

"He overworks and there are months when I never see him. He holds his offices of Constable of England and Warden of the Marches too much in conscience. He must learn to delegate authority. God knows he has loyal gentlemen enough. Young Percy, Frank Lovell and Ratcliffe to say naught of the devotion and good sense of his secretary, John Kendall."

Summoned to the Chamber of Presence somewhat early one day Catherine found the Duke seated at a table. He had been working but was now engaged in conversation with a soberly attired man, whom he'd courteously invited to sit in his presence. Catherine had noted that he rarely kept people standing or on their knees. Once she had heard him speak feelingly of the weariness of the long hours in attendance at Court and wondered if he were sometimes more tired than he would admit. If this visitor was a messenger he had been welcomed with undue kindness for she saw a wine-cup at his elbow. She made her curtsy and waited until the Duke explained his purpose for calling her to the chamber. Was there some instruction from the King concerning her? She stifled an unreasoning fear. She had no wish to leave Middleham yet awhile.

"Mistress Catherine, I would like you to greet our visitor. He is your cousin and is numbered among my household. Since he is kin to you I wished to present you formally. He has been on business on his estates. Sir Hugh Kingsford, this is your cousin, Mistress Catherine Newberry."

Catherine almost stumbled as she swept the man her curtsy. He had risen when the Duke spoke, to greet her. His voice was deep, his delivery slow as if he considered carefully before uttering any words at all. He was over-tall, topping her by over a head and a half, and she considered herself high for a woman, preferring the lower, smaller hennins now they were in fashion. He had bowed to her and as he stood upright she regarded him curiously. He would be at least thirty years of age, perhaps he looked older than he was, for two wide silver wings of hair framed his brow and temples. Gloucester had introduced him as one of his household, so presumably he was a soldier, but he looked every inch a scholar or clerk, save for his plain soldierly attire of brown woollen doublet and grey hose under a leathern jerkin, much roughened by hard wear. Yet she noted there were heavy seal rings on each hand and he wore a gold and enamelled chain, odd decoration she thought on apparel untrimmed by fur or embroidery. He was thin to the extent of cadaverousness and his face was long, his expression almost lugubrious, but there were traces of humour apparent round the eyes and mouth which suggested that when this big, dark man did condescend to smile it would light up his whole countenance. A small scar had winged his right eyebrow, possibly an arrow graze, and, slight as it was, it lent the man a rakish air, almost diabolical. Prepared to hate him with relentless intensity, she found herself strangely at a loss in this encounter. Gloucester was continuing to speak.

"Sir Hugh is a widower, Mistress. His wife died five years ago in child bed. He is left with two small daughters who lack the care of a mother."

The allusion was deliberate and Catherine's lips tightened involuntarily.

"Good day, Sir Hugh," she said quietly.

That smile came and readily. The tiredness left the long dark face and he bent to kiss her fingers.

"My Lord of Gloucester has told me much of your situation, cousin, for I hear we are distantly related. I am grateful to the Duke for his care of you."

"You hold our lands, I believe," she said as deliberately as the Duke's cool suggestion, "I shall be pleased to hear from you later concerning the welfare of my former attendants."

If she had hoped to embarrass him her shot did not succeed. He nodded gravely. "I shall be pleased to wait on your leisure."

Gloucester had listened to their exchange without moving. Now he waved Catherine to the door.

"Sit with Sir Hugh at meat, Catherine. Now I have business to discuss with him. Seek out the Duchess. I believe her to be in the nursery."

Outside, having descended the keep stairs at a run, Catherine found herself shaking with frustrated anger.

Did they think her a tool to marry her so conveniently to this ageing widower who held her lands and needed a protectress for his children? Her chin jutted obstinately. Had the man the effrontery to believe that he could acquire her dower as well as his property, rightfully hers? They would find her a tougher nut to crack. The Duchess had promised her she would wed where she would. She gazed across the Court to a group of lounging squires, resting from their practice with sword and dagger, preening themselves under the gaze of two giggling maids from the dairy and feeling themselves scrutinized from above, where Bridget Ransom drew herself hurriedly back from the casement. She must wed and if not with Kingsford with whom? He was eminently suitable. Gloucester had made that clear. Had the man already agreed to take her? If so she knew she had little chance of refusing the match, whatever the Duchess had said.

In the nursery Anne was occupied discussing with nurse the prince's diet for he had lacked appetite of late. She greeted Catherine absently and later Catherine felt she could not overburden her mistress with her anxieties concerning the new arrival. For the present she must keep her own counsel.

CHAPTER IV

The sudden early heat had lessened by late May and the latter part of the month had been dull and cloudy, but with the new moon the sky cleared and the ladies and younger knights and squires prepared to make the best of the finer weather and ride out with falcons and picnic. The youthful prince had received his father's gift of a pony; docile though it was, the lad was delighted and anxious to exercise his mount and show it to advantage.

The Duchess too seemed pleased to leave Middleham, visiting local gentry and the religious houses round about where the Abbesses were always delighted to have her patronage.

Kingsford remained at Middleham. As Gloucester had commanded Catherine had sat with him in Hall and accepted his determination to seek her acquaintance. He was not a courtly wooer, but he was no fool and she came to realize his worth in Gloucester's household.

The Duke and Duchess, with a small train of attendants and accompanied by the Prince, were returning to Middleham from a day of falconry. It was early June and a fine, warm day. The Duchess quickly tired of the sport, since she had distaste to see the falcon swoop on its prey, and surrendered her hawk to the falconer. They rode leisurely and at last the Duke drew rein near some meadow land and declared his intention of resting here for refreshment.

Attendants hurriedly spread a cloth on the grass and provided fine white bread, cold meats and wine. The Prince greedily ate his fill, his appetite had returned since expeditions from the Castle had resumed. The Duchess watched him fondly while she toyed with the food herself. Gloucester stretched himself some short way off beside Sir Hugh Kingsford and Sir Francis Lovell. They were obviously enjoying some scandalous tale since Catherine could hear their sudden bursts of laughter, where she sat in her place near the Duchess. Bridget chattered on regardless that the Duchess was becoming tired.

"Go off and walk awhile," Catherine whispered. "She needs to rest. Take the Prince. He is restless, but first ask the Duke's consent and take a squire with you."

Bridget scrambled to her feet, brushing down her skirts. She was only too ready to fall in with Catherine's suggestion. Catherine called for cushions from one of the sumpters and Anne sank back to rest, her eyes watching the retreating backs of young Edward, Bridget and two watchful squires with some relief.

"They will be safe enough together. Won't you join them, Catherine? I am fatigued by the ride but I am well attended. My Lord is close."

"No, Your Grace. I am a little tired too. I'll stay with you and laze here in the sun."

The Duchess slept while Catherine smiled at her peace. Lately she had worried about the lad but he had recovered. He would sleep well tonight if he ran and amused himself awhile. The Duke was relating. Recently he had been closeted in Council late into the night.

A messenger had come hot-foot from Court. Bridget had repeated scraps she had from pages. The lads spent their days with their ears half pressed to doors. The King's Grace had again become displeased. The Duke of Clarence had been refused the royal permission to seek the hand of Mary of Burgundy, the dead Duke's daughter by his first wife.

" 'Tis said the Duchess Margaret encouraged Clarence," Bridget imparted with relish, "but the King forbade the match and the Duke sulks on his country estates. Now he is enraged since the King offered an alternate suitor for the lady, Lord Rivers."

Catherine had smiled. She would have been a witless fool had she not known how matters stood between the King's second brother and the Woodvilles. The antagonism between them had near wrecked the Yorkist cause.

"Of course Will says that Rivers was rejected," Bridget went on, "but there has been some further scandal. He could not hear. The Duke was very grave when he received the missives and seemed anxious to keep the news from the Lady Anne. Will caught some mention of the Lady Isobel. They would not wish to renew her grief at the death of her sister."

Catherine had been puzzled. Isobel of Clarence had been these long months in her grave so what could occur now to so concern Gloucester?

She looked across at the lounging group. Hugh Kingsford lay somewhat apart. Her eyes caught his studied gaze. Furiously she turned away and snatched at the daisies near her feet. As if on cue the wanderers returned. Catherine was glad of it. She felt the need for some break in her sudden depression of spirits.

Young Edward was chattering with his father and Bridget came bounding back to the Duchess, her skirts tucked up and a light basket in her hand.

"Strawberries, Your Grace, the very first of the season. The farm woman said they grew near to a sheltering wall in the garden and had come on so early with the unexpected heat of last month."

The Duchess sat up and turned back the snowy napkin. "How lovely and Dickon loves strawberries. Did you pay her well, Bridget?"

"She would take nothing, Your Grace. She says the Duke was excessively merciful when her youngest boy was brought before him last year on a charge of poaching. The lad could have hanged or lost his hand. Apparently he got only a reprimand and a sound beating."

The Duke strolled across, the young Edward trying desperately to keep pace with his stride.

"Then I must order more beatings if I'm to receive such rewards," he said smiling down at them. The child had an armful of summer flowers.

"The lady gave me cake with honey and these flowers for my mother and the ladies." He almost fell in his haste to present his mother with his trophy.

Anne reached out to rumple his hair and touch with appreciative fingers the mass of blooms in her lap, columbine, stocks, monks-hood, late rosemary, spiky yellow flowered broom and two or three early and perfect rose buds.

"Darling, how lovely. Did you thank the lady?"

The Duke smiled down at his son. "So she gave you sweetmeats? And who explains to Nan when you are sick? Remember your instructions. We must divide the spoils of campaigning with the ladies."

He leaned across and selected a bloom as Anne turned laughingly to Bridget to choose a nosegay.

"For Mistress Newberry, our little nun, one perfect white rosebud." He offered the flower with a flourish.

Scarlet with anger, without thought, Catherine beat up his hand.

"I do not want it — will not take it."

The stem flew from his fingers and, in stooping to retrieve it, he cursed roundly as the thorn drove deep into his thumb and blood marred the whiteness of its petals.

There was an anxious silence. Anne stared at her wonderingly. The Prince, conscious that he had some part in this scene and unaware of its significance moved awkwardly backwards, stumbled and fell against Sir Francis who lifted him to his feet and stood, one arm round his shoulders, supporting him.

The Duke held out the flower imperatively.

He was rigid with anger. His mouth had hardened into a tight line.

Catherine reacted blindly. Subconsciously she knew she had committed an unforgivable sin, insulted the House of York, rejected the Duke's gift, a studied act of discourtesy. No one spoke.

She said through gritted teeth. "It is spotted with blood."

"Royal blood, Catherine. A Prince bleeds to please you." He spoke very softly. "Take it." The final words were a command.

Slowly she lifted her eyes to his. His grey-green ones blazed. She forced her lips not to tremble as she rose and backed from him, placing her hands deliberately behind her back.

"Your Grace will excuse me. I am Lancastrian. I have never sought to hide the truth. You knew it when you took me from Gupshill."

"Yet you will show respect. Take the rose."

"No." Her courage was fast ebbing but she jutted her chin obstinately. "My father died for Lancaster. I will not deny the cause if it means my life."

"It may mean a sore back." The Duke's tone was even.

The Duchess gave a strangled gasp. A cloud had crossed the sun. The pleasure had gone from their leisurely afternoon.

"Dickon, the lass is upset." Frank Lovell's voice came pleading, as if from a distance.

"She may be but she is under my jurisdiction and she will obey. She is not too young to be taught courtesy."

Despite the warmth of the sun, Catherine felt suddenly chilled. Tears threatened to spill down her cheeks, try as she might to prevent them. The Duchess was pleading wordlessly for her to accept and patch up the breach of the spoiled peace. The Prince was shivering unaccountably and Gloucester did not take his eyes from her.

She gave a strangled gasp and gathering up her skirts ran from them blindly. Kingsford sought to bar her way but with the cunning of desperation she avoided him. The tussocks of grass flew up before her face. Roots and small twigs lay in wait for her unwary feet but somehow she remained running. The grooms and attendants were dozing beyond the horses.

She reached them panting and desperate, without assistance pulled herself into the saddle of the first available mount. She felt the thin stuff of her gown tear as she did so and tugged, blind with hot tears, at the rein tossed over a branch. Then she heard the sound of a shout behind her, and dug her heels into her mount's soft belly. Unused to such feminine handling it reared and almost threw her. Grooms stumbled, startled to their feet, half-witted with sleep.

Her mount gave a snort of rage and tore off across the meadow, Catherine clinging wildly to its mane. She was an excellent horsewoman but this mount was beyond her ability to control and she was in no condition to think coherently. Blind with panic she tore at the reins and the beast, maddened by her attempts, galloped faster. He took a hedge at speed. Catherine felt herself hurled above the saddle but somehow managed to stay mounted. The horse now was careering across meadowland and towards a small copse of trees. Realizing the need to let it have its head now until it quietened of itself, Catherine continued to hang on grimly. She gritted her teeth and her panic having cooled, considered. The trees would slow up her mount's head-long gallop but there were added dangers. She must lie low in the saddle as low branches could drag her down or even decapitate her.

Her gown tore further as she set herself to crouch low as the animal tore into the shade of the thicket, her heart pounding to the rhythm of its hoof-beats. She had been right in her surmise. Without open country to encourage her mount to faster speed it slowed down somewhat. Still she knew to seize the bridle rein now would be a mistake. The animal would react violently and this she must avoid at all costs.

Then she heard the sound of pursuit. She could not turn to discover if one or more of the Duke's gentlemen were behind her. Her panic was renewed and she made no attempt to take the chance the slackening of speed afforded. She dug in her heels hard and the beast once more reared in fury, then catastrophe — a rabbit or vole startled by the animal's whinney of anger sprang across its path. Awkwardly the horse stumbled and fell. Fortunately Catherine was thrown clear though she was flung against the thick bark of an oak. Agonizing pain shot through her right arm and she gave a cry. Mingled with her shock was the added fear that she might have harmed the horse. She struggled up, knowing her pursuers were close. If the horse's leg was broken she would be in further disgrace. God — what would Gloucester say and do? She felt sick with terror and pain.

Arms caught her in an iron grip as she fought vainly to free herself and continue her escape.

"Lie still, do you hear me, lie still, God damn you."

The Duke's voice cut across her panic.

Dully she continued to fight him.

"Beat me, kill me, I don't care — I don't. I will not take the rose. The horse —"

"Catherine!" The Duke's voice was hard with concern rather than anger. "Lie still. You are hurt. I will not harm you. What a little fool you are. By the Saints, we thought you'd be killed."

Despite her efforts to free herself he laid her back against the tree's sturdy trunk, and spent, she rolled over, weeping bitterly.

Firmly he turned her back, his fingers probing the damage to her arm which hung limply. she cried out once as he touched the source of the pain.

"Thank God, your shoulder is unharmed. I thought —" He broke off and, bending, tore further at the ruin of her gown. "The forearm bone may be broken. We must let the surgeon examine it further. I'll bind your arm to your body. Lie quiet now and do not fight me. It may hurt but I'll be quick."

She bit back the cry as he tied the wounded limb in two places. Her tears spilled down her face, ploughing grubby furrows through the sweat of fear and pain which had drenched her whole body.

"Why did you follow me — why? —"

"It's fortunate I did since you might have lain here for days untended."

His fingers reached up to her forehead and she winced under his touch.

"You've a lump like an egg, but since you're conscious there's no great harm. Don't try to move. You're shocked. We'll get an improvised stretcher and a litter. You'll be safe enough. Are you cold? Shocks chill the body, I've experienced it often with wounds after battle."

She shook her head but he noted that her teeth chattered and cursed inwardly that the day being warm, he had no cloak to wrap round her. Abruptly he removed his blue velvet doublet and placed it round her shoulders. "Better? They'll find us soon. We scattered in the search. The ground is so hard it wasn't easy to trace you." He grinned. "Lovell will be not a little concerned for his mount."

She controlled her shivering. "Is it — hurt, My Lord?"

He glanced up and then grimaced down at her ruefully.

"He's pulled a muscle, I think, but I doubt the leg's broken. God help you if it is. Frank prizes the brute above rubies."

Tears poured down unchecked, realization of her utter stupidity and grossly insulting behaviour now making itself fully felt.

"Your Grace, what shall I do? I was so foolish. You baited me and it was all so sudden. Please —"

He touched her uninjured arm gently.

"It was my fault, Catherine. You are not used to my teasing and I taunted you deliberately."

Her eyes widened as his lips twitched.

"But why — I do not understand?"

"You have over-done the submission, Catherine. I confess you puzzled me. 'Yes, Your Grace. No, Your Grace, anything you command, Your Grace'. I am a fair judge of women, Catherine, and I doubted that even six years in a convent could have wrought such a change in Newberry's daughter. You've intrigued me. Just once or twice you've let me see the real Catherine. Today I tested you. I wanted to be sure."

"Sure?" Her voice was husky with unshed tears.

"Sure that you have not forgiven me and to be careful that I guard myself."

Her face whitened and he grinned again.

"Rest easy, Catherine, I am a just enemy, I make no war on women and children."

She stared at him wordlessly. Not since that terrible day in the market at Tewkesbury had she felt so utterly drained of emotion, all the fight in her gone. He put out a hand as if to touch her, then he stiffened, his lips tightened involuntarily and he sat up again. As if in answer to his need for action, they heard the sound of hoofs and men calling.

"They went this way, Sir Francis."

Gloucester rose and went towards the entrance to the clearing.

"We're here, Frank."

Kingsford and Lovell rode hastily up and dismounted. Sir Hugh's anxious glance went to Catherine's huddled form by the tree. Lovell looked at her quickly then went to his limping mount. Gloucester said briefly to Kingsford, "She is safe but the arm may be broken." He called across. "Is the hurt serious, Frank?"

"No, thank God, he's sprained his left foreleg. With rest it will heal itself."

"We'll get the farrier to poultice the joint."

Gloucester moved to where Sir Francis, kneeling, was gently feeling the injured limb. "You are fortunate he stumbled and rolled over. He could have broken his back and Catherine's too."

Lovell nodded and stood up. "What's to be done, Sir?"

"Can one of you ride back and fashion me a stretcher?"

Catherine struggled to her feet, before Kingsford could aid her, limping towards them. She gave a further grimace of pain. Her ankle must be injured too for it gave her excruciating pain when she set her weight on it. "My Lord, I could mount with assistance."

Gloucester nodded approvingly. "Hugh, if I mount will you lift her up to me? Frank, you'll want to lead your horse more slowly. Kingsford will take the bridle of your borrowed horse."

Kingsford lifted her gently and Gloucester drew her back into the circle of his arm. "Come closer, Catherine, your arm will jar less painfully."

She felt herself held against his chest. She still wore his doublet round her shoulder and was painfully conscious that she had imposed upon his dignity, though he seemed unaware of the odd sight the Duke of Gloucester made in his shirt sleeves, a dirty and bedraggled girl held on his saddle pommel. He urged his mount forward slowly.

"Hugh," he said, over his shoulder. "I'll head straight for Middleham. Will you go back to the Duchess, call off the search and come on with the party?"

As Kingsford rode off immediately to obey him, Catherine sought to control her trembling. Once before she had ridden thus, frightened and hurt, against the protection of his body. Her thoughts were once more in chaos. He had sensed the hate in her, but was it so? He roused in her a tangle of emotion, but now as they rode on without words, until Middleham came in sight, she could not believe that hatred was at the core of her hurt. It was something else and it terrified her more than the pain which would soon come when the surgeon set her arm, or the terror of punishment, nor yet the indignity of staring eyes and whispering tongues. As they passed under the gatehouse, she was aware that her primary concern was that he might send her from him.

CHAPTER V

The Duke's physician, Dr. Hobbes, set the bone while Gloucester held her firm against the bed head and the Duchess stood anxiously by with a cloth soaked in lavender to wipe her brow. Catherine could only hold back her screams by gritting her teeth so hard she thought she might damage them, but she would not play the coward in his sight. When it was over she sank back against the pillows, exhausted and drenched in sweat. The physician pronounced himself satisfied, having splinted the limb, that it would set of itself in time and without distortion. He left a bitter tasting draught to relieve her pain and allow her to sleep.

The Duchess dismissed Bridget and the Duke left with the doctor. Anne sank down on the bed and assisted Catherine to drink.

"Now you must rest quietly and not worry. All will be well," she said gently pushing back the sweat-drenched strands of Catherine's ash-blonde hair, now that they had removed her torn gown and her ruined hennin. The Duchess and her ladies had reclothed her in a clean shift and rubbed healing salve into her aching body.

"I have removed Bridget to sleep in a small apartment in the Keep," she went on, "until you are better." She smiled. "She is such a chatterbox. She means well, but you cannot cope with her yet awhile. Are you in pain, Catherine?" This last as hot tears poured down now, splashing on to the fresh linen sheets smelling sweetly of lavender and rosemary.

"Your Grace, I am so sorry to have caused such a trouble after all your goodness. It was unforgivable to refuse to take the rose only —"

"Catherine, you must not think of it again. The Duke should not have teased you so." She handed the weeping girl a clean handkerchief of cambric. "There is no harm done. The farrier says Frank's horse will be as well as ever. My Lord can be very Plantagenet sometimes," she nodded as Catherine's eyes widened. "Do you understand what I mean? I am sure you do. So often he is friendly and casual and always courteous and now and then, he becomes royal and prickly." Her blue eyes became warm and soft, her mouth tender. "There are times when I am brought up sharp against the facts that I married Proud Cis's son. You see how I trust you, to talk with you so."

"But you love him?" Catherine's question was whispered.

The Duchess turned from her, her voice dreamy.

"I have always adored him. He was seven when he came here first to Middleham. He was such a dark, gaunt, withdrawn little boy for his father and brother had only recently been slain after Wakefield and they took George and Richard into exile for a while. Then after Towton and Mortimer's Cross and Edward ruled in Westminster, the boys came here to squire my father, the Earl.

"George was always the lively one, tall and golden-haired, and with such charm everyone spoiled him. Isobel ever had more confidence than I had and so Richard and I were left apart and as I watched him from a distance, forcing himself to wield heavy sword and battle-axe, despite his slight build, I knew his will and his courage were stronger than George's, stronger than Edward's, stronger even than my father's." Her lip quivered.

"Then the King and my father quarrelled after" — she hesitated — "after the King married Lady Grey. It was dreadful for him, you must understand, since he was engaged in arranging a royal match for the King with the Princess Bona of Savoy. He was mortally insulted and my father was not easily crossed. The King sent for Richard and it was long before I saw him again and it was never again possible for us to talk with our old intimacy."

There was a little silence and Catherine was afraid to break the Duchess's mood by an intrusive question.

"They married me to Edward of Lancaster while my heart broke for Richard. My father railed against him that he would not support our cause but Richard's motto is 'Loyalty Binds Me' and I knew he would never desert Edward and York."

"The Prince — ?" Catherine could not refrain from prompting the Duchess to reveal her own feelings of a loveless match.

"Poor boy, he was never allowed to become true man. Though Margaret treated me ill, I felt for her agony when he fell at Tewkesbury." Anne plucked at the bed coverlet. "She would not allow him to consummate the marriage until my father had won England again for her. I did not complain. He was a strange boy, half effeminate, half monster, always talking of battles and thinking of cutting off men's heads. Yet he was gentle enough and courtly when she allowed it. She had the worst of it in the end since there was no heir for Lancaster."

She turned back and regarded Catherine

gravely as the shadows deepened in the little room.

"Do you not think I feel for you, Catherine? My own father was slain at Barnet and my loyalties divided. Clarence took me into his home and he wished me dead." She made a little expressive, hopeless gesture of her hands. "I escaped from his house but there was nowhere to go, no one I could trust. You see I knew your plight, I'd experienced it, that is why I pleaded for you to come here to Middleham."

"But could you not trust Gloucester?" Catherine's voice was incredulous.

"I couldn't then. There were tales, ugly, stark rumours. Some said he slew the Prince when he appealed to the Royal brothers for mercy. Then the King died, Harry of Lancaster, and he was at the Tower that night —" She broke off. "I should have trusted him, known that he was not one to stoop to defend himself from malicious, spiteful tongues. He expected me to believe in him and I failed him."

"I took refuge in a cook shop." She shuddered. "I do not think I can remember much about it. I was ill and they treated me badly. Richard's squire found me there. I think the place was a brothel though I had not understood in my ignorance. He fetched Richard."

"And all was well?"

"All is well." The Duchess bent to tuck the sheets round Catherine's bruised body. "He did not force me to the match. He left me in the Sanctuary of St. Martin, and at last we were wed and came to Middleham. Now I have told you my life's history, you must sleep. I tire you."

She stood up. "Roses are beautiful, Catherine, red or white, remember that." At the door she paused. "And they both have thorns, sharp and deadly." Then she was gone and Catherine was left to stare upwards at the raftered ceiling, her thoughts in turmoil.

She had inveigled herself into Middleham with the express purpose of harming the Duke. To do what she planned would destroy Anne of Gloucester and she knew now she could never do that. Yet her distress was greater. Hoist in her petard, she knew she loved him too, as deeply as the little Duchess, and entirely without hope.

It was blissfully quiet without Bridget, during the next two days, though she crept in, anxious to perform any required service, or to entertain Catherine while the physician kept her to her bed. The ladies spoiled her, even the dour Countess visiting her chamber with some sweetmeats to tempt her jaded palate. Left to herself she gave way to the weak, ridiculous tears that came so often, these days. She was disgusted with her own folly, but despite her urging, could not bring herself out of this state of self-degradation.

Once over the shock, the physician gave permission for her to rise and seek entertainment in the household, but awkwardly without the use of her right arm she was valueless in the Duchess's service and not fleet enough of foot to be sent on errands. Unable even to strum the lute or occupy herself with her embroidery, she roamed the courtyard, disconsolate, or sat near the windows, her fingers for once idle, staring over the castle precincts and the town. Even the battlements were denied her as Gloucester sharply warned her the stairs were too winding and steep for her to climb in her debilitated state.

Feeling thus disheartened and wholly neglected she sat one afternoon in the Great Hall, idly turning over the pages of her Book of Hours, the Abbess's gift from Gupshill and examining the Duchess's beastiary, a volume much admired by the young Edward. The household had ridden out, but Catherine could not yet handle a mount so she was unable to accompany the Duchess and the Countess of Warwick had taken to her bed, complaining of a blinding headache, the result of sitting out in the hot sun of yesterday.

She had dismissed Catherine who had offered to remain in attendance, and left to her own devices she felt strangely depressed. It was shaded in the Hall, but drowsily warm out of doors and she felt the servants and attendants had sought their pallets to doze away the afternoon.

From the Chamber of Presence Gloucester abruptly emerged and stopped short on seeing her there.

She rose and curtsied low. "Your Grace, I had thought you with the hawking party."

"No," he said shortly, "a messenger came from the Court. I needed to remain behind and read the dispatches. Then there were answering letters which needed immediate attention." He passed a hand over his brow as if his eyes ached from the strain, though she judged that worry concerning the text of his replies to the King was at the core of his trouble. He sat down in an armchair and looked round the Hall.

"Is there no page about or are they all with the Duchess? I could do with some wine."

"You are tired, Your Grace. I will withdraw and send a servant to attend on you."

He waved his hand towards a wine flagon on the dresser. "Be my page, Catherine. Can you manage one handed?"

"Yes, Your Grace."

She handled the flagon and wine cup with care and brought it to him. He sipped appreciatively and then sat peering down into the glowing liquid.

"Are you recovered? Does your arm pain you?"

"I am better, sir, and conscious that I owe you a sincere apology. I was discourteous and foolish."

One eyebrow rose sardonically. "We have said enough on that. The affair is forgotten. Sit down on the stool. Since you are here there is a matter to discuss with you."

She held her breath in sudden dread, but obeyed him.

"While at Westminster I made enquiries concerning your father's immediate effects —" he paused, looking closely at the design of his wine cup and avoiding her eyes, "his armour, horse, any jewellery on his person."

She said quietly, "I thought such effects became the property of the headsman."

He was silent for a moment then resumed. "Sometimes. In this case the worth was able to be estimated. In these last dispatches the King's secretary informed me of the amount. It is sizeable. I had thought you would care to use it in some way personal to yourself, to buy some jewel to his memory, since his own rings and chain were disposed of, or for masses at the Abbey or even to build some fitting memorial. Sir William's grave is unmarked. Perhaps a brass — I could arrange it."

She could not think for a moment what to reply. She was close to tears again. She said huskily, "I think I would like to see Sir Wilfred Newberry's name recorded in the Abbey. Would the cost be too expensive, sir, if so, I could wait —"

"Did you say, Sir Wilfred?" His voice was unaccountably sharp. "Your father was Sir William Newberry of East Lulworth?"

Her eyes widened and she frowned. "My father was Sir Wilfred Newberry of Newburgh Manor near Gloucester. I told you that time in Tewkesbury. We are distantly related to the Newberrys of Lulworth but there was some quarrel, I think. My father never told me the details. We bear the arms, bends azure, but —"

She broke off as he was obviously not attending to her final words. The wine cup had tilted and spilt wine on the woven carpet. He sat still watching the scarlet drops mar the bright threads of its pattern. She sat still, her eyes also riveted on the blood-like stain, slowly spreading.

"My father was mistaken for another?" Each separate word was jerked out slowly. It was not possible that he could tell her that.

"Catherine, can you remember your father fighting any earlier campaign, leaving the manor, visiting Norfolk or the North?"

She shook her head blankly.

"Think now. You are sure?"

She nodded, her lips pressed tight together.

"In the Abbey — was he wearing some surcoat, some rag of standard? Can you remember? You saw him before — ?"

"His arm was injured. I think he had a scarf. It may have been embroidered with our arms — I — don't —" She gave a sob, low in her throat. "They butchered my father by accident." She spat out the word. "That is what you are trying to tell me. That is it — isn't it?"

He leaned forward into the chair, the wine cup dropping to the floor, his hand reaching to catch her shoulder as she made to rise. "It is possible. I will not hide the fact. Sir William's name was among those indicted for the Redesdale risings. He had been one of King Edward's gentlemen, sworn to our cause. Later he abetted Warwick. My brother Clarence identified him in the Abbey."

"But he could not have done. My father never saw the Duke of Clarence before that day, I swear it."

"Then he was mistaken. Perhaps the arms —"

"And Sir William?"

He shook his head wearily. "I do not know. He may have been among the slain. Certainly he did not survive the battle." His voice was very gentle as he said, "It was as Sir William Newberry I judged your father on the King's express command, and in that name I condemned him."

"But why was he given no opportunity to defend himself?"

"Catherine, he made no effort to do so. Perhaps, like us, he was confused. He had fought for Lancaster and been defeated. He believed himself guilty of the charge as made against him. He said little to justify himself. There were so many and they were all silently courageous, supporting the might of Somerset."

As she fought to rise and run from him he held her to the stool and dropped on one knee before her.

"He was proud to die for Lancaster, Catherine. You must believe that. It was quick and clean. God knows I would run mad if I could not assure you of that. Ask any man who fought that day if he could be sure he struck no comrade. Errors are made in the heat of blood-fever. Your father would have understood. Cry for him, but do not poison your mind with hate for me, little one. If I am guilty of spoiling you, turning your splendid woman's gentleness to bitter heartbreak, my crime is more heinous than when I sat in judgement on your father."

She was crying now, her hands pressed to her mouth to suppress the terrible tearing sobs which would proclaim her shock at the enormity of her discovery.

He tried to draw her taut knuckles from her lips.

"Please, Catherine, do not hate, I beg of you. It will destroy you."

He was holding her wet hand and she strove to check her weeping. "I cannot hate you, My Lord. It is impossible." He bent to catch the choked word. "My father must forgive that I love his judge, for I do love you."

His fingers tightened on her hand and he placed his free hand against her trembling lips. "No, Catherine," he said, his voice hard with the effort to remain calm, "no, you do not, cannot love me. You do me great honour and I am deeply moved, but, my child, you are beside yourself with grief and shock and cannot know what you say. I was foolish to broach a subject which could give you naught but pain at a time when you are still shocked from your injuries. Now, Catherine, try to dry your tears and sit in this chair. I will get you wine. It will strengthen you and then I'll find some woman to attend you. There must be some suitable female to help you now. They cannot all have gone from the Castle."

She sat huddled in the chair while he went to the dresser for the wine. His hand was firm as he raised it to her lips. He would accept no denial and she gulped at it and felt the liquid course through her.

Her hand was steadier when she returned the cup.

"I am sorry. I should not have spoken."

He took his time crossing to the dresser and replacing the cup. When he came back to the chair, his expression was grave.

"I think it is time we provided you with a husband."

"You will send me away?" She was pleading and he passed his hand again over his eyes as if to shut out the sight of her.

"It would be wiser so."

"I could go to where you send me, some cottage. There would be times when you could come, My Lord, I do not ask for your love, only a place in your affection."

"Catherine, you have that."

"I wish to bear your children. I —"

He turned abruptly from her and she knew she would have bitten back her words had it been possible.

His voice came as if from a distance. "I love my wife."

"But there have been others — you have children —" Her voice trailed off uncertainly.

"They were conceived before I married Anne, when it seemed possible —" he hesitated, "that I would never do so. I have touched no woman since."

"But she is sick. There must be times when —"

She quailed under his fury as he turned back on her, his face thunderous. She groped desperately for some glimpse of hope.

"My Lord, I beg of you," she broke down then under his impassive silence. "You are commanding me to wed Kingsford?"

"He is a good man, already attracted to you. It would be a marriage of some substance. You would be well provided for. I believe — he would be good to you."

"He is old."

His grimness relaxed beneath her wail of protest.

"He is twenty-six, some seven months older than I am."

"Please don't make me. Let me stay."

"I will not force you to wed against your will but I shall send you away. I must."

She stared out of the window stonily. "I would not hurt her. She will never know."

He said harshly, "She *must* never know."

There was silence. He had gone apart from her as if her nearness would endanger his determination.

She rose and faced him, but his back was turned from her.

"You send me because you will not trust yourself. If you had no feeling for me you would not have brought me here or sought for me in the wood. You will not touch me now."

He said icily, "I will not hurt her, and I will not hurt you. You have my reasons. It is enough. You have my permission to leave me, Mistress Newberry."

She curtsied low and he acknowledged her obeisance with a courteous nod. At the door she turned back for one last sight of him but his attention was given to some person in the courtyard, for he was leaning to look from the window.

She went down the stairs with care and when she reached the bridge which connected the Keep with the South apartments in the South Wall she heard the sounds of return as the hawking party streamed into the castle ward. She ran then to her own chamber, barred the door and gave her grief full rein.

CHAPTER VI

Excusing herself attendance at supper, pleading indisposition, Catherine kept to her own chamber. She could not bear to see the Duchess in the Hall beside her husband, nor was she fit to make idle converse with Sir Hugh Kingsford.

When Bridget knocked timidly she was stretched on her pallet in silent misery, her tears exhausted. The child's pretty head was thrust round the door and Catherine saw she was deeply troubled.

"Catherine, are you better? They said you were sick."

"Yes I am. I felt very tired. My arm pained me. What is it?"

"Oh Catherine, could you come to the Duchess's chamber. She is greatly distressed. I think I heard her sobbing. My Lord Duke is closeted in his chamber with Lovell and Kingsford. I dare not disturb him and the Countess is still abed. I do not know what to do or say to comfort her."

Catherine rose instantly. "What grieves her? Is aught wrong with the Prince?"

"No. He is in the nursery. He seemed in good spirits after the ride. His health gives no cause for anxiety."

"I will come."

Bridget gave a sigh of relief and hovered anxiously while Catherine adjusted the silk sling Dr. Hobbes had ordered her to wear to keep the limb at rest.

"I am grateful. I never seem to know what to do at such times."

As they crossed the court Catherine asked tremulously, "Was the Duke with her earlier? Did they quarrel?"

"He was with her." Bridget's face seemed pale, her brown eyes limpid with concern. "I do not think he chided her for aught. You know he is always gentle with her."

Catherine nodded. She paused near the Duchess's chamber. "Leave me with her, Bridget. I'll send if she has need of you."

Gratefully the girl sped off and Catherine approached the door. She could hear no sound of voices so she judged that the Duchess was alone and tapped discreetly.

There was a pause. The Duchess's voice sounded faint and a little thickened. "Who is it?"

"It is Catherine Newberry, Your Grace. I am recovered now and willing to attend on you. Is there aught you require?"

"Come in, Catherine."

The Duchess was kneeling at her priedieu. It was clear that she had been weeping. Her face was deadly pale and her eyes puffed and swollen.

"Your Grace, are you ill?"

"No, not ill." Anne allowed Catherine to help her up and seated herself at the foot of the huge bed.

"What ails Your Grace — ill news from court?"

Anne nodded. "Sit down, Catherine. You are a good girl and will not gossip. It is best you know."

Catherine said softly, "Does the King send for My Lord of Gloucester? Is there war?"

"I pray God it does not come to that. Richard is not summoned but I think he will go South if there is need, but Percy sends word there is trouble on the border and he feels his place is here."

Catherine's thoughts raced to Bridget's whispered comments. "There had been news concerning the Lady Isobel, which would grieve the Duchess." Why? Isobel was dead.

"His Grace of Clarence has arrested a woman of our household. In our youth she attended both Isobel and I. Her name is Ankaret Twynhoe. She had given devoted service to my sister, Isobel, but recently she left to live in Somerset. Clarence's men broke into her house and hauled her off to Warwick. I cannot believe — he charged her before the magistrates with my sister's murder, and she is hanged — drawn on a hurdle and hanged."

Catherine was frozen with horror. The Duchess of Clarence murdered? There had been no talk of such. Surely she had been sick of an infection of the lungs and had weakened during her late pregnancy, dying in childbed.

"But, Your Grace — I thought —"

"He accused her with a serving man, Thursby, of poisoning Isobel. It could not be. Ankaret loved Isobel as she loved me. Both protested their innocence. Ankaret swore that Isobel was not in Warwick on the day in question but in Tewkesbury. My Lord was white with fury, they said, and the magistrates afraid. They condemned them both."

"Your Grace, I am deeply shocked and I know this has revived your grief but you must try to be calm. This can do no good. The Lady Isobel is dead and it seems that naught can be done for her servant."

Anne stifled her tears. "There is worse. Richard has known this for days, it seems, and sought to spare me. Now couriers bring word that the King is enraged by Clarence's action. He had no right to try the woman.

She should have been judged by the King's officers."

"Then why —"

"It is all of a part. Clarence is mad. He thinks the Queen's kin suborned Ankaret and Thursby to murder Isobel and the new born infant."

"But it makes no sense."

"Of course it does not but until Ned's boys were born Clarence was the acknowledged heir. Why do you think my father wed him to Isobel in the teeth of the King's opposition? Clarence is close to the throne. He has always desired it. Recently Edward has ailed. Clarence hoped again — a minority, George in power. His own sons were also heirs. Can you not see why the King is so hot against him? This act of Clarence is directed at the King and his wife."

"My Lady, is it possible? The King has heirs and My Lord of Clarence has an elder boy."

"Little Edward is backward and has been since birth. We hoped he would develop. It was for this that Richard wished to see him and little Margaret in Warwick. Clarence neglects the boy and Isobel has been so sick of late she could not give them the love and care which our Edward has always had. Richard believes a child needs to know the love of his parents. He has never sought to take little Edward from me, into the sole care of nurses and attendants. Why, even the other children he visits often —" she broke off, putting a trembling hand to her mouth.

"I am afraid, Catherine. It seems the King has made a counter charge. He has accused one John Stacey of having worked witchcraft against him at the instigation of Thomas Burdett of Arrow, a servant of My Lord of Clarence. Another man, Blake, has also been arrested and put to the question. They have confessed. Poor souls what else could they do? They told how at sundry times they had made leaden images of the King and melted them to bring about a like wasting of the King's body." She was silent then she said, horrified, "They have even said My Lord of Clarence knew of this and Isobel also before she died."

"The King would not believe such a terrible thing of his own brother."

"They are both mad with hate each for the other. I believe George is moon-mad. He rails against Edward, against me, against Richard. He has even stated openly that he holds true that spiteful rumour that the King is no lawful son of the dead duke but a bastard of the Duchess's begetting with an archer called Blackburn."

Catherine caught back a gasp of fear. It was clear that the little Duchess was beside herself even to breathe such dangerous treason here in this room to her attendant.

"Come to bed, Your Grace. Try to rest. Leave this to My Lord. He will know what best to do to protect the good name of Her Grace, your sister. I will summon the doctor. He will give you a soothing draught. You must sleep."

As she emerged from the room she encountered Gloucester. She curtsied, afraid to lift her eyes to his face but his voice was level enough as he courteously acknowledged her greeting.

"The Duchess is beside herself, Your Grace." She spoke softly and hurriedly. "I am going for the doctor."

He checked with his hand on the door and she explained. "She needs something to help her sleep. She knows not what she says. Guard her and watch yourself."

His eyes flashed. He had read her warning correctly. He bowed and moved into the room.

The doctor was found and went immediately to the Duchess's apartment. Bridget started up from a stool in the hall but Catherine shook her head at her gently. She sat down with a nod. The hall was noisy with chatter. A squire was humming some plaintive air and further off two pages were dicing. She could hear the chink of the dice in the wooden cup. She paused beside the Duke's secretary, John Kendall, who was playing chess with Sir Richard Ratcliffe. As usual Kendall was winning. Ratcliffe grinned at her ruefully, then gave his attention to the board. It was hot here and the air over-laden with the smell of stale food and perfume. She half stumbled over two hounds snarling over a bone in the rushes. She felt a gentle hand steadying her elbow.

Sir Hugh Kingsford said quietly, "Allow me, Mistress Newberry. You must not again become injured."

She flushed. "I thank you, sir. I need air. Will you excuse me?"

He said evenly, "May I escort you?"

She hesitated but only for a moment, then she inclined her head. "If you will be so kind, Sir." They left the hall together.

There had been a rainstorm early in the evening which had cleared the air and laid the dust in the courtyard. From the Duchess's small pleasurance came the scent of columbine and stock. Bouts of weeping had given Catherine a severe headache and she drew in the night air thankfully. Still it was warm enough to linger out of doors and though now quite late, the lighted brands flared evenly, throwing the shadows into stark relief.

Kingsford said, "I would speak with you, but if you would care for me to have a woman near by —"

"No need, sir. I cannot distrust your motives."

"Then I may speak?"

She nodded and he paced slowly at her side.

"They will have told you that I have asked for your hand?"

"I think, sir, the Duke of Gloucester bade you ask for my hand."

He did not seek to evade. "It was suggested to me as a worthy match."

"And is it so?" She faced him squarely.

His dark face was troubled. He made a little expressive gesture with his hands. "I am older than you but not so old. I will consider your wishes. I owe you that much. I own your lands. They will again be yours and I have no heir. The child of your body will inherit the manor. Is it not fitting?"

"My father would have wished that." Her voice was very low.

"I will not expect too much of you."

She smiled. "I cannot love you, Sir Hugh, now or ever. Will you accept that?"

He did not speak and she said again, "Can you?"

"There are loveless marriages in plenty. My own —" he broke off. "We were children and we grew apart. I sense a vital force in you, a spirit I have not known in woman. I could learn to love you."

"That might be unwise." She walked from him to the gatehouse. The porter dozed on his stool and she went out across the drawbridge, looking over the green towards the swine-market. She felt him close at her elbow.

"Will you consider, lady? Could you take me, breed heirs for me?"

She turned. "I do not need to consider, sir. The Duke of Gloucester commanded it. It shall be as he wishes."

He made to touch her but she drew apart.

"Then I will have the marriage contract drawn. We are handfast?"

She nodded and he reached out and held her hand. For some minutes they stood silent, then she withdrew hers gently.

"You will love my children, I think. Cecily is nine, an obedient girl. Janet is five. She cost her mother her life but Ellen ailed from childhood."

"I am sorry."

"I shall wait impatiently. Unfortunately I shall need to delay the marriage. I must soon ride South on Gloucester's business. It will give you time to prepare your dower chests and —"

"Sir Hugh, will you grant me one favour?"

"If it is in my power."

"Will you wed me at once and take me South with you?"

He frowned, his lips a little parted as if he were astounded at his own good fortune.

"I should be thankful to do so. I think the Duke will consent but there are problems."

"Need they be insurmountable?"

"I think not but you will want your wedding to be celebrated fittingly and I must ride with all speed to Windsor. The journey would tire you."

"I am no delicate flower. I can ride hard and fast. My arm is almost recovered."

His cheeks flushed under his normal pallor.

"Then there is naught to fear."

"You will speak with Gloucester?"

"Tomorrow." He stooped towards her. "May I kiss you, coz?"

She nodded and steeled herself for the touch of his lips, light as the wing of a bird against her forehead.

CHAPTER VII

Catherine peered upwards into the blackness. The curtains of the bed enclosed her with her husband in a world apart from the bawdy noise and merriment away in the Great Hall. Even now, far into the early morning, she could hear the faint sounds of it. She stirred only faintly to touch the cold metal of the wedding ring on her hand. Hugh was sleeping evenly at her side. She felt the nearness of his long hard body and was careful not to rouse him.

She wished she did not feel so empty, so completely without emotion. Tonight had proved Hugh did indeed love her and that in the inmost recesses of his heart he hoped that what she denied him now might one day be given. He had been gentle with her and she was grateful. She knew too that to some extent her own flesh would play her heart false. She would respond to Hugh's love-making, and not merely because she felt it incumbent upon her to do so as his lawful wife, but because it pleasured her. She frowned, perplexed. The Chaplain at Gupshill had railed at lust and was not the delight of love-making without love — truly lust? Was she then at heart a whore? It could well be for she would be ready enough to surrender her body freely to Hugh while her whole soul longed for Gloucester.

He had been gracious when Sir Hugh spoke of their need for haste. Her eyes had sought his, appealing. If now he would speak, make opposition, delay the ceremony, she would still hope, but he had not done so. He acknowledged, quietly, that since Catherine's injuries were now almost healed he saw no reason for withholding his consent. They would be adequately protected on the journey South and he knew well Mistress Newberry's skill as a horsewoman.

Anne had regretted lack of time for adequate preparation but Catherine's dower chest was already packed with the fashionable garments she had scarcely worn, so there was no need for bridal clothes. They were to be wed in the Chapel of the Keep and would leave the next day on Gloucester's business. To some extent Catherine thought that though Anne expressed doubt at parting so soon with her new and favoured attendant, she would not entirely regret the departure. She had spoken more freely than was safe and it would be wiser, in the future, if she was more reserved in her dealings with her women. Bridget Ransom would not be an acceptable confidante and she would not again be so easily tempted to reveal her inmost doubts and fears.

Despite its hurried nature Gloucester had called the local lords to do honour to the bridal pair. She had gone into the Chapel on his arm and she did not tremble when she laid her own upon it. His eyes smiled his pleasure at the match, though his mouth was tight as once before she'd known it and she thought he held it so, to betray no pain or doubts of the outcome.

She had not again spoken with him alone. Had she wished it, she could have made opportunity but it was pointless. She knew the strength of this man. He had decided and he would not waver from his resolve. She understood. Anne adored him and needed him. Other wives accepted the inevitability of their husband's faithlessness. Anne worshipped Gloucester and though she would endure a knowledge of a favoured mistress without complaint, part of her would die. She was gentle with his bastard children, visiting them at Sherif's Hutton, becoming actively interested in their progress and schooling but she had no rivals in their mothers. Gloucester loved her and her alone and in the warmth of his affection she had bloomed again at Middleham, but it was a fragile flowering and unexpected frost would wither and destroy it.

So Catherine had gone smiling to her marriage, her hair unbound and garlanded with flowers, the bridal knots sewn lightly on her white silk kirtle fought over merrily by her companions. Hugh's hand reached out and took hers where they sat in the Great Hall, the trestle heaped with the choicest of dishes. The cook had grumbled loudly at the Duke's lack of thought in not giving ample warning for the feast, but as usual, he excelled himself, and she was honoured with as brilliant a banquet as any princess.

She was exhausted by the dancing. Gloucester led out the bride, but the galliard was too energetic for her to more than speak hurried conventional phrases of thanks. When their hands touched it was all she could do not to scream aloud her agony at his cruelty in thus giving her to his gentleman. Soon she was partnered by Lovell, Ratcliffe, Lord Scrope; indeed Hugh had much ado to exert his right to dance with his bride at his own wedding feast.

They undressed her and placed her naked in the great bed, combing out her long blonde hair and strewing the room with the sweet-smelling herbs with their symbolism of fertility, and they had both endured the bantering and shameful lewdness of the bridegroom's party which accompanied him to the chamber. Then the Duke's chaplain blessed them and the curtains fell into place and they were alone together.

She smiled at him in the glow from the night rushlight, glimmering from the pricket on the table near their bed. The curtains there had been left undrawn, that he might see his bride.

"I hope, sir," she said shyly, "I shall not give you cause to regret your choice."

He smiled crookedly. "Nor I disappoint you, madam."

He put out a hand and touched a lone strand of her hair. "In this light it is almost silver. You are indeed lovely, my wife."

She let him fondle her and he wooed her gently so that she relaxed in his arms, not the cold rigid statue she had feared she might be, and at last he had slept, content, but sleep had evaded her, and she lay throughout the night viewing again and again the events which had led her to his arms.

She bit her lip, regarding his shadowy form thoughtfully. So far he had treated her well but at Tewkesbury he had done her mortal ill and she must not forget that Gloucester's disclosures concerning her father's fate had strengthened her resolve that this man too was involved in that betrayal. Clarence had been careless, Kingsford had known what he did and because her father had died, and none had spoken in his defence, his manor was now Kingsford's. She had failed in her wish to harm Gloucester, or had she? Was he indeed so content in his stronghold here at Middleham as he had been before he brought her here? What was her intent for Kingsford? Would she, *could* she punish him, or was her decision to wed him one devious way of achieving her own ends. At least he was to take her South to Windsor and later London. One fact at least was crystal clear. South she would see Edward, the King, and unless the fates deserted her, his brother, Clarence.

As the grey light stole between the overlapping bedcurtains Kingsford woke, stretched and turned to look at her.

"Did I wake you?"

"No, I was already awake."

His voice was contrite. "Have you not slept? I thought not to hurt you, Catherine."

She turned her head to him. "You did not, sir. I am content."

His arm encircled her shoulder and she let him draw her close. "Gloucester has given me leave to detour into Leicestershire. We have little time but I would have you see the children."

"What are they like?" she said dreamily,

her fingers tracing the lines where his shoulder bone stood up gauntly over the valley of his throat and the hard flesh of his chest.

"Both dark, though Janet favours her mother, praise God, more than Cecily who is like me."

"Your elder daughter must feel the lack of her mother."

"Aye, the more so since her own nurse died soon after Janet was born. The new woman is efficient enough but Cecily appears to bear her little affection."

"I pray that she likes me."

"She will, sweet. Her heart cries out for love and there is little jealousy in her."

"But will she not resent the fact I take her mother's place?"

He shrugged faintly, his own fingers now entwining two ropes of her hair together.

"I think she can scarce remember Ellen. She was but four and even before that Ellen ailed when carrying the child. She has seen little of me either since for the most part I have been away at Barnet and Tewkesbury and in the Scottish border country on Gloucester's marches."

"I will try to make her like me."

"If she resembles her father, that should not be difficult."

He sat up abruptly. Even in the gloom of

the tented bed, the arrow graze stood out sharply and she wondered fleetingly if he had taken vengeance for its getting on the executed Lancastrians, or had he acquired it on some earlier campaign?

"Catherine, you do not regret?"

"No."

"What I said before — that I had not asked you in love. It was clumsily put. We shall deal well together. You will not have cause for complaint. Already I —"

She put out two light fingers and barred further speech. "Say nothing more, sir. We have an understanding and an excellent arrangement. I will serve you as wife to the best of my powers, and I pray God grants me a son, more I will not promise."

He bent and kissed her hard on the mouth, then drew from her, his fingers lingering on the polished splendour of her young white shoulders and the firmed roundness of her breasts.

"Possessing you is all I ask. Gloucester amply repaid any service I did him when he summoned me here and suggested the match."

He had swept back the curtains then and reached for his bed-robe or he would have felt the sudden rigidity of her whole body. She waited motionless, until he went from her, then turned on her side and for the first time since Gloucester's denial, allowed herself the final refuge of tears.

Despite the early departure the whole household was assembled to speed Kingsford on his way and to wish his youthful bride happiness and fertility. She declined to ride in the litter, though Hugh pressed her, and he gave way in the end and ordered her palfrey saddled. The Lady Anne kissed her warmly. Marian hugged her, tears brimming her pansy-dark eyes. Catherine waited while Hugh talked apart with Lovell and Ratcliffe. Even from here she could see Frank Lovell's expression was unwontedly grave. So this affair between the King and Clarence was indeed a matter of urgency and it was most probably for this Gloucester sent Sir Hugh to Windsor with personal dispatches.

She looked in vain for him. She stifled her near panic. He must come, he must. Agony though it would be, she could not ride out from Middleham without a last glimpse of his loved form. Was he engaged in his chamber with Kendall? But he would not allow Kingsford to leave without bidding him "God Speed", yet she knew such sentiment was ridiculous. The Lord Constable had weightier matters to engage his attention than to wish a member of his household well. Hugh had his orders. There was no need to enlarge on them.

Margery Whittacker, the maid the Duke had engaged for her on their ride North, in Coventry, was to accompany her. She was a good-hearted simple woman, blowsy of appearance and with little courage, but efficiency in service which belied her looks. She had become more used to riding now and to living in close proximity with the men-at-arms with their lewd tongues and rough and ready ways. She was berating two of them roundly as they loaded Catherine's dower chests on to the patient sumpters.

The groom brought up her mount and assisted her into the saddle. The men mounted and prepared to move towards the gatehouse. Hugh swung himself into the saddle with a wave of farewell to his two companions in the Duke's service. He rode forward to her side.

"You are ready, everything packed and loaded?"

"Yes."

He peered forward anxiously. "You sound fainthearted. Would you, after all, prefer to remain here until I return? It is a hurried arrangement. The Duchess would have no objection."

Her heart gave a great lurch but she forced

herself to remain calm and smiling.

"Of course not. My place is with you now."

He smiled his relief, his dark eyes lingering over her slender beauty.

Then she saw Gloucester at last silhouetted against the open door of the Keep. Behind lumbered burly John Kendall.

"My Lord of Gloucester." Hugh rode to the foot of the Keep stairs and made to dismount.

Gloucester came down easily.

"No need, Sir Hugh. I could not allow you to go without my good wishes. I was so busy with preparations for the expedition to Northumberland I had overlooked the hour." He clasped Kingsford's hand. "God speed you. Send me word when you can."

"Aye, sir. Be assured I will do all circumspectly."

"I know that. I trust you well. You're a fine soldier and what is better you've a discreet tongue and a good head on your shoulders."

He came towards her then and she saw the early sun tinge his brown hair with red glints. He reached up for her gloved hand and she surrendered it, the other clutching tight at the bridle rein so that momentarily her horse reared.

Gloucester smiled. "Stay on his back, mistress."

"I promise to, sir."

"Hugh will not object if I kiss the bride. I had no time to take my prerogative yesterday." He moved closer and she lowered her head for his formal kiss.

It came hard on her mouth and her lips parted under his, then he withdrew smilingly. "God keep you safe, Catherine, and give you all you desire."

She said softly, "God will not do that, sir. It would not be good for me."

"No." His mouth was suddenly tender. "That is true."

She forced her mount forward slowly as Hugh moved to the van of the little procession. Once over the drawbridge she turned. He stood easily, his arm round the Duchess who lifted her hand in farewell. Catherine turned abruptly, tears threatening to choke her.

It could not be possible that she had spent so little time at Middleham. Here her whole life had changed. She had become a woman and a wife and here within these frowning walls she left her heart.

Once clear of the town Hugh rejoined her. It was warm, but not unpleasantly hot, early June, a time for strawberries. She would ever remember that Gloucester loved strawberries. She half listened to Hugh's talk. He was anxious now to prepare her for her sight of his

Leicestershire manor, near the village of Cadeby. The children lived there in the care of their nurse.

"It will be for you to decide where you wish our more permanent household to be. Doubtless you would prefer to be established at Newburgh, since it was your childhood home. During these last years I've been in the saddle more than at board. It will matter naught to me."

"What? Oh, I'm sorry, Hugh, I was dreaming in the sunshine. By all means settle our children where you wish."

He nodded content and she thought later it was the first time she had considered Hugh's daughters as her own, or of the heirs she might bear him.

CHAPTER VIII

Hugh's manor was small and snugly nestled among the gentle, rolling lands of the Midlands. After the harsh bracing air of the Northern Dales it was smiling countryside.

"I hold the land as tenant under the Lord Chamberlain, Lord Hastings," he had explained. "He is planning to build a new home here at Kirby." He laughed. "Fortunately there is no need to fortify with such care here in the Midlands. We are less close to the coast and fear little from border forays. I shall knock down the outer walls of the manor land and extend the court in time, also build on to the keep if we intend to stay here."

Kingsford was a small squat keep, surrounded by a dry ditch and protecting wall, against which nestled the outbuildings. After Middleham it seemed dwarfish and ill-appointed, but her welcome was warm enough. The manor attendants were obviously pleased to receive their lord's young bride and cheered their greeting.

A tall gaunt form waited near the door, her hand holding tightly that of a small chubby girl. A second girl stood anxiously by her side. Catherine stooped to embrace the younger girl, but, rising, her eyes sought those of Hugh's elder child.

She curtsied as she had obviously been schooled. "I bid you welcome, mistress. My father's outriders brought us the news two days ago, ahead of you."

She was, as he had said, like him, unusually tall and clumsily angular with the awkwardness of girlhood. Her dark hair was drawn back smoothly from her brows and secured with a ribbon. She wore no coif and she was fast outgrowing her kirtle of green wolsey linsey. It did little for her dark complexion, Catherine thought. She must take the child's dressing in hand. The younger, Janet, clumsily clung shyly to her nurse's hand and drew away, alarmed, when her father sought to lift her into his arms.

"They grow, Mary," he said delightedly. "You have cared for them well."

The woman curtsied dutifully, her cold blue eyes surveying Catherine with careful attention. It was clear she viewed her new mistress with some suspicion, understandably, since she had ruled here for so long with undisputed sway. She ushered them within for refreshment.

Hugh ate quickly and rode off with his steward to view the estate. They had so little time before resuming their journey South. Catherine took the opportunity to retire to their chamber to rest. Though she disliked to admit it, the pace of their travelling had tired her.

When the timid tap came, she sat up. "Come in."

Cecily paused in the doorway, uncertainly.

"Come in, child. Did you wish to speak to me?"

The girl closed the door carefully before coming nearer to the bed at Catherine's invitation.

"Come here, on to the bed near me. We must get to know each other."

The girl hesitated then did as Catherine bade her. She seemed ill-at-ease, lacking confidence. Catherine had noted that she did not speak throughout the meal unless deliberately addressed by her father.

She had been little more than this child's years at Tewkesbury. How would this timid little scarecrow have faced the sights of those days?

Cecily swallowed. "Do you think you will like Kingsford, madam? I hope you will."

"I think I shall. It is fine farming country and good for hunting and hawking, I imagine. Do you ride much?"

"Very little. Mary says she has the responsibility for my safety and she cares not for outdoor pursuits. Janet claims all her attention. Once or twice she has given me permission to ride with a groom, but I leave the house rarely."

"Are there children nearby for you to visit?"

"No, madam."

"Then you are too lonely, Cecily. When I was your age I was in a convent in Gupshill. I had many friends. We must remedy the situation."

The girl regarded her with piercing insight. "My father says you may go to live at Newburgh."

"Yes, that may be so. It was my father's land and I love it. I have not seen it for six years."

"Will you —" the child swallowed again, "will you leave us here with Mary?"

"Not unless you wish it." Catherine smoothed back the dark hair. "I cannot take your mother's place, Cecily, but I can be your friend. Our ages are not so different. Soon you will be presented to the families of the local gentry. I shall need to prepare you for society."

"In the convent did they teach you worldly matters?"

Catherine laughed. "Yes. I think I was polished for society viewing better than if I had remained in my father's house. I was motherless too and I ran free of the manor like the boy my father had hoped to have."

"My father is disappointed in us. He wanted an heir."

Again Catherine detected a note of unusual gravity, rare in so young a girl.

"And if I give him one, will you resent it, Cecily?"

The girl's lips parted in a little gasp. "No, madam."

"That is good." Catherine touched the ugly kirtle thoughtfully. "Have you finer clothes?"

"No and I am growing out of all my gowns. The seams are splitting. Will you talk to father?"

"I will and I promise I will bring you silk and ribbons from London and perhaps a lute. Do you play, Cecily?"

"No. Oh madam, will you teach me?"

"Certainly, and many other arts. Do you sew well?"

"I think so, and I ride my pony. Wat says I've a good seat." Her face fell. "How long will you be gone? Do you know?"

"Some time. Your father rides on the Duke of Gloucester's business to the King at Windsor, then to visit the Duke's mother at Baynard's Castle. We carry gifts for her."

"I wish — I wish —" Cecily broke off and

laughed. "Oh never mind, but send for us soon, please, please send for us soon."

"What did you wish, Cecily?"

"That I could go with you," the child's tone was wistful.

"London is no healthy place in the summer, child. Though I have never been, I know that well."

Cecily nodded then scrambled from the bed. "You are not angered that I disturbed you?"

"Of course not."

"I must go. Mary will say that I have tired you and my father will be angered."

Catherine nodded and the girl slipped away. Catherine sank back against the pillows and thought about the state of affairs at Kingsford.

That night by Hugh's side she tackled him on the subject. He was drowsily satisfied. Several times on the journey she had been forced by circumstance to sleep apart from him and he was glad tonight to hold her in his arms.

"You cannot continue to neglect Cecily's education. The child lacks company of her own age and will be awkward when the need comes to make a suitable match for her."

He grunted. "Time enough."

"She dislikes the nurse."

"Yes." He gave a sigh that they must discuss

this now. "I feared as much."

"She would like to go with us."

"I imagine she would." His tone was comically indignant.

"Is it so outrageous a request? She has seen little of you. You have confessed it."

"But Catherine — take the child to Court?"

"She need not be presented. We shall be in lodgings. You will be busied. I would welcome her company."

He sat up, peering down at her.

"Are you serious? This is what you want?"

She considered. "I wish to win her confidence. The sooner the better. Think about it, Hugh. The child will need a complete new wardrobe. In London I can deal with everything and we shall not be there long enough for evil humours to threaten her health. She seems strong enough."

"Aye, she rarely ails."

"If there's plague in the city we could stay at Windsor."

He lay back heavily. "Very well. God knows you are in the right of it. She seems a very yeoman's daughter. It's time you licked her into shape."

Catherine was satisfied. Once in control of Hugh's elder daughter her position in the household would be strongly established. She settled herself to sleep, since there would be extra work to do before they could depart in the morning.

Windsor was hot and crowded as Hugh had expected since the King was in residence, however his dispatches, sealed by Gloucester's own hand, afforded him the attention of the stewards and to his surprise he was eventually summoned to the Lord Chamberlain's apartments. Lord Hastings, as debonair as ever and considerably weightier than when Hugh had seen him last, greeted him cordially.

"Welcome, Kingsford. How is His Grace of Gloucester? I hear you carry personal dispatches for the King's Grace."

"My Lord is well as is the Duchess and the little Prince. Yes, sir, I have orders to carry my letters to the King's hand in person. I understand it will be some time before I can obtain an audience but I would be grateful if you can expedite matters for me."

Hastings waved him urbanely to a chair and called a page for wine.

"I hardly think His Grace will keep you waiting. He is ever gracious when his brother has urgent business for his attention." His eyes were narrowed despite his jovial manner and Hugh wondered if he guessed the nature of his business. Already he had heard that on 20 May My Lord of Clarence had stormed into the Council chamber, the King being absent, incoherent with fury, protesting at the condemnation of Stacey and Burdett, and demanding that the King be moved to hear his plea of innocence. Edward, when told, had gone livid with anger. Stacey and Burdett had been hanged at Tyburn and Clarence's ill-advised action at approaching the Council without first consulting the King, had further enraged him. He had sent a terse command to Clarence to remove himself instantly from Westminster until commanded to appear before him and the Duke had withdrawn to Warwick to sulk and drink himself into a stupor while his tongue did not cease from clacking to his intimates of the shameful way he had been treated.

Hastings asked after former companions who were at Middleham in Gloucester's service.

"The quarters in the castle are not commodious, I fear, but I could provide you with a corner. The King will wish to have you close at hand."

Hugh murmured his thanks. "My Lord, I must explain I have recently remarried and my wife accompanies me with a maid and my elder daughter."

Hastings clapped him soundly on the shoulder.

"Right glad I am to hear your news, man. Is she pretty and wealthy?"

Kingsford coloured. Knowing Hastings's propensity for the fair sex he was determined to keep watch over the youthful Catherine.

"She is sixteen, very lovely and the King's ward. So hands off, you lecherous dog. I know you too well to leave her out of sight in your company."

Hastings took no offence. He roared with laughter.

"You intrigue me, my friend."

"Her father was a Lancastrian gentleman, Sir Wilfred Newberry, slain after Tewkesbury. She had been at Gupshill nunnery and the Duchess of Gloucester requested to take her into the household at Middleham. She had a fair dower, but I am fortunate. When you see her you will understand."

"I am indeed delighted. It's long since Ellen died and you need an heir." Hastings leaned back in his chair. "Aye, well, you'll need apartments. That may be more difficult."

"I can take lodgings in the town."

"I'd not advise it. Leave all to me. I'll inform His Grace of your presence and provide accommodation if I can."

Hastings was as good as his word. The Kingfords found themselves in possession of two tolerable chambers at the rear of the castle. Though Hugh roundly cursed at the beggarliness of their appointments, Catherine had expected less and Cecily was too entranced by the new delight of being with them to see aught amiss at sleeping on a truckle bed in a small room she must share with Catherine's maid, Margery Whittacker. Kingsford's squire, young Will Tollerton, was sent to find his own sleeping place with the squires and other pages of those attendant on his Grace, probably in the Hall with the lesser servants. The boy was even-tempered and expressed no ill will at the arrangement and they settled themselves patiently until the King saw fit to summon Hugh to his presence.

It came earlier than imagined. Within hours Hugh was summoned to the King's private chamber.

When he returned she was relieved to see that he did not appear dismayed. He bent to embrace an excited Cecily. "Your stepmother and I are ordered to dine in the Hall so we shall be excessively late. We shall try not to disturb you."

Catherine's eyebrows had risen at his tidings. "Did all go well?"

"Excellently. His Grace was extremely affable."

"Did he read Gloucester's letters?"

"Immediately. He seemed to accept their

sentiments. He quizzed me about my bride and, as you heard, I am to present you tonight. God, but I wish we'd had more time to rest and prepare. These court functions are wearying to the stoutest heart. Will you bear up?"

"Certainly, sir." She flushed. "I had not thought to be presented. I shall enjoy the experience."

She dressed in a gown of blue brocade and wore a small hennin trimmed with cloth of silver. She regarded herself critically in the travelling mirror which had been Anne of Gloucester's parting gift. She looked somewhat pale and a trifle drawn. Recently her mouth had taken a slight downward pout since her accident in the copse near Middleham. Her arm had knit quickly and she no longer needed to wear the silk sling. She disdained the need for any cosmetic, contenting herself with licking her finger and sweeping it across her fair eyebrows, smoothing any stray hairs and patting smooth the band of silver-fair hair showing from the front of the hennin.

Hugh looked well in murrey and blue, the Yorkist colours. He settled his gold chain as he stood behind her and gently squeezed her shoulders.

"The King will have no fault to find."

"Do I look a dowd?"

He gave that slow smile at her anxiety.

"You do not, but somewhat nun-like." He chuckled. "His grace is said to prefer holy women." As her eye brows flew up in comical distress he stooped and kissed her cheek. "Nay, 'tis a rare jest, sweet. Heed me not. Do not be afraid to speak out if addressed. He is no ogre, our Ned."

Accustomed to feasting at Middleham, Catherine had not expected to feel so strange. She sat mid-way down the hall with Hugh where a flurried steward seated them and hardly dared lift her eyes from her plate. Course after course was served as the wine flowed faster and the talk grew louder and more bawdy. Hugh was soon engaged in converse with his neighbour while Catherine sipped at the sweet Malmsey, for once, at a loss.

When a steward whispered discreetly in her husband's ear, he touched her arm lightly, and she knew the moment had come for her to look on the face of Edward of England for the second time.

She felt all eyes upon them as they advanced to the throne-dais. She swept a low curtsy, hardly daring to lift her eyes to the King's chair.

"We are pleased to welcome you to Windsor, Mistress Kingsford." It was a pleasing voice, less musical than Gloucester's but pleasant and without undue querulousness or arrogance.

"I thank Your Grace."

She looked up as he had risen and was leaning down to assist her up the steps to be nearer his person. Gorgeously apparelled he was as splendid as ever. His fair, almost auburn, hair curling on to his shoulders, his features handsome, his blue eyes boldly appraising. It was his mouth that gave the lie to the languorous easiness of manner. It was wide, full lipped, sensual enough, but the set of it betrayed a determination and shrewdness which would not draw the line at deliberate cruelty to secure a given purpose. His lips lingered unduly on hers in the formal kiss of greeting.

"Well," he said smilingly indicating that she was to occupy a chair by his side. "So this is the young lady our brother has exhorted me to provide for. You have been fortunate in the match, Kingsford."

Hugh bowed. "Your Grace, I am aware of it. My Lord of Gloucester assured me you would hold no objection to the marriage."

"Indeed no, it seems an admirable arrangement especially since you have provided us with the opportunity of meeting our ward in person."

"My wife preferred not to wait until I returned from my errand, Your Grace."

The King's eyes raked over her. "Did she? Hot for you, you dog? God knows, Kingsford, at our age we cannot always expect such a gift from Dame Fortune. How long will you stay at Court, mistress? We hope to be favoured by your company some months at least."

There was a faint gasp from the group nearest the throne and Catherine coloured hotly.

"I will be here only as long as my husband is engaged in your service and that of the Duke of Gloucester, Your Grace, but I thank you for your graciousness."

"Bess, do you hear?" He appealed to the Queen who until now had lounged indolently beside him. "We had hoped to provide you with an extra lady in attendance."

Aware that the King's invitation implied favour beyond the normal degree of courtesy, Catherine eyed her from under her lashes. She betrayed no irritation. Still a regally beautiful woman, Elizabeth Woodville had long learnt to accept the evidence of her husband's infidelity, even if it were paraded before her face. He had taken her from the obscurity of widowhood, when her dead husband had been his enemy, married her in the teeth of opposition from his nobles and the influential members of his family, and though he constantly strayed from the path of virtue, he never ceased to treat her with affection and courtesy. He came to her bed when it suited him and she had given him beautiful children.

Like the King she was clad magnificently in scarlet and cloth of gold and appeared perfectly content. Behind her were her elder son, Thomas Grey, Marquess of Dorset, stepson to the King, and her brother, Lord Rivers, who had only recently returned from Ludlow where he was preparing the castle for residence of the young Prince of Wales whom he was to take into his charge.

She smiled at Catherine. "I would willingly accept you among my ladies if your husband approves."

The King cut across her words. "Since we have messages for our mother the Duchess of York at Berkhampstead, Sir Hugh will have no objection, we are sure, if his young bride remains here with us at her leisure. Our need being urgent, he will oblige us and it would be unfit to submit so lovely a young creature to the rigours of travelling again so soon in this heat. Do you not agree, Hugh?"

Hugh's lips twitched as Catherine looked at him uneasily. "Your Grace is considerate as ever."

"Will tells us your daughter is here."

"Aye, sir. I have seen so little of her of late, Catherine persuaded me to allow her to accompany us. I fear her head will be turned by the excitement of this early taste of Court activities."

"Nonsense, man, the sooner the better. We will visit your apartment and see her for ourselves."

Catherine caught back her breath as she saw Hugh's mouth tighten but again he bowed and remained silent.

"So you were educated at Gupshill?" The King's hand beckoned a page forward and handed over his wine goblet. "Do you dance, mistress?"

"A little, Your Grace."

He rose. "Will you partner us?"

She complied at once, rising, though her limbs trembled.

He was a superb dancer and partnered her splendidly. It was a stately slow movement and his hands lingered, palm against her palm, as they met, then drew apart in the pattern of the dance. He had thickened considerably since she had seen him stalk commandingly into the Abbey at Tewkesbury, but he had not run to fat. Still he was England's golden giant and she knew that many female eyes envied her as she paced at his side.

The dance having ended, his fingers grasped hers firmly. "It is over-warm, mistress. Will you come with me to the terrace for air?"

It would be impossible to refuse for he led her with gentle but firm insistence and the courtiers drew back to give them passage.

The cool air of the gardens was a welcome relief from the perfumed heat of the hall and she breathed in the scent of the night-stocks thankfully. He steered her towards a bench and waited until she sat. She peered round anxiously and he laughed.

"There are attendants close enough for propriety. Are you afraid of me, mistress?"

He had dropped the use of the royal pronoun and she looked up at him enquiringly. His blue eyes mocked her.

"No, sir," she said evenly.

"Do you fear Hugh's reprimand?"

"No, sir."

"At least you make no idiotic excuses for seeking to end our talk. Tell me of Dickon and Anne. Are they well — and little Edward. They tell me he is as delicate as ever."

"I think the Duchess is much improved, sir, and the Prince. He is learning his skills with sword and bow avidly. He is a bright child and well advanced at his studies."

He frowned. "Is he? I think my Ned is lazy and little Dickon an artful monkey at

avoiding work — as for George's Ned —"
He broke off abruptly.

"The Duke of Gloucester is as active as ever in Your Grace's service."

"Aye," he whispered. "I'm blessed by one fine brother. I trust Dick with my kingdom, my children and my life."

As if he felt some intuitive prompting of her loss, he said quietly, "He was good to you, I think. Were you sad to leave Middleham?"

"I was very happy there." Her voice quavered only a little. "His Grace has treated me with extreme kindness. He placed me at Gupshill and arranged my future."

"And Hugh pleases you?"

Her eyes met his frankly. "He will be good to me and since he holds my father's forfeited lands, I am grateful for his care."

"He's a good man, Hugh, if somewhat stolid." He laughed gaily, "and so serious. We can wait for an hour to see him smile but" — he leaned forward peering into her face — "perhaps you have given him cause to smile more often. Is there yet promise of an heir, mistress?"

"No, sir."

"You're sure?"

"Perfectly, sir."

He leaned back, but, taking her hand,

traced the fine bones of her slender fingers with his own index finger heavy with its seal ring.

"You'll not fret to accompany him? I meant what I said. I need him to ride for me to my mother, and to the Council."

"He is at your command, sir, and I will serve the Queen if you bid me."

"Will you want to go soon to Middleham?"

She hesitated and averted her head. He could not gauge her expression. "No, sir," she said. "I shall not return to the North. The air will be chill in the winter for Cecily and young Janet. When Hugh goes to Gloucester I shall stay either in Leicestershire or at Newburgh."

"Or at Westminster," he prompted gently.

She lifted her eyes to his. "At Westminster if Your Grace wishes it."

Lord Hastings's voice came smoothly at their rear.

"Your Grace, the Archbishop wishes to take his departure, with your leave."

"Stillington? Oh, aye, Will. We'll return to our duties."

Smilingly and without haste he led her back to the hall and released his grasp of her fingers as Hugh, bowing, came forward to take her arm.

"My ward appears to have profited by her

training at Gupshill, Sir Hugh. We shall be pleased to see her often at Court."

As he moved off toward the Queen's side, Catherine kept her eyes lowered.

Hugh said nothing concerning the King's monopolization of her company either then or later in their chamber.

CHAPTER IX

The King kept Kingsford at Windsor for the next two days. During this time he insisted that Gloucester's messenger hunt with him and Catherine was requested to join the party. She revelled in the chase but found, since her sojourn at Gupshill, that she had developed a distaste for the kill. The Queen kept to her apartments complaining of the heat.

Hugh was ordered to Berkhampstead on the third day. Since the King's marriage the Duchess of York had frequently withdrawn from her London home at Baynard's Castle into the seclusion of the nunnery.

Cecily bade him a hasty farewell and darted into the corridor to talk with a young lady-in-waiting. As yet the King had not come to their apartment to visit the child privately as he had promised.

Hugh dismissed Margery Whittacker and embraced Catherine.

"You will not be gone long?"

He shrugged. "I think not, two — three days at the most. Do not over-tire yourself."

She moved languidly from him to the bed.

"I am weary. The dancing lasted late into the night."

He grunted. "You are much in demand as partner, since His Grace honours you."

"Hugh, do you censure me?"

"No, since it would be ill-advised to refuse but —"

"You wish me to plead indisposition while you are gone. Keep to my chamber?"

He made a little helpless gesture. "No, it would avail us nothing." He turned to go. She arrested him as he reached the door.

"Hugh —"

He swung round slowly and she read the fear in his eyes. "Make no promises, Catherine. I ask none. God keep you." Then he was gone.

She bit her lip in sudden anger. Was he a witless fool that he saw nothing of the way the wind was blowing? Edward made no secret of his interest. He made her presents of his hunting trophies, partnered her each evening. She had not been unaware of the Queen's amused, almost contemptuous regard. That she was already the focus for gossip she knew well. The Court marked her as Edward's new fancy, indeed probably believed that she had in fact surrendered to him. Why he should single her out was a puzzle. Her beauty was unremarkable, though she had extreme youth and freshness as her principal accomplishments, both rare at Court. It was clear she was inexperienced and she had little skill in the art of witty badinage. She neither encouraged nor repulsed the King. Since Hugh had never spoken of his feelings in the matter she could not know whether she would please him by her submission or anger him by refusal. Her face burned with the slight of her humiliation. Hugh would accept his position as cuckold to his royal master without shame with as easy a conscience as he had apparently taken her father's lands. Well, since he cared not, she could ill afford to keep her reputation by angering both the King and her husband.

Perversely she kept to her chamber. Hugh had been banished on the King's errand so that Edward could have a free hand with his wife. Could she doubt it? She fumed at the thought. Anne of Gloucester had sworn that she would not be sold in a shameless match. If this were not, what indeed could be called so? She had thought he might command her presence, but no word came. Margery fussed over her.

"It is the unrelenting heat and I have been fatigued by the feasting and hunting. I will take this opportunity to withdraw from the Court while Hugh is absent."

Cecily sat by her side soaking handkerchiefs in rose-water to ease her aching head. Indeed Catherine had not lied. Her head did ache abominably and she had sickened at the rich foods in the Great Hall.

As the evening wore on she sent Margery and Cecily to bed as the child was beginning to wilt. The maid undressed her and left her in bed with her book of hours, and some embroidery nearby. Even the bed-robe seemed over-heating and she drowsed, allowing it to fall open and her body to cool once the maid had gone promising to come immediately if Catherine called her.

She must have slept for she woke with a start to almost opaque darkness in the room. Some sound had alerted her. She sat up, putting aside the curtain to reach for the tinder-box to light the night candle. A hand firmly clenched over her mouth to stifle her cry of alarm. The candle sprang into flame and she saw Edward smiling by the bed-side. He released her mouth and she sat back, pulling the bed-robe more tightly around her. He was fully dressed though his blue velvet doublet was undone and she saw the soft whiteness of his fine cambric shirt beneath.

His eyes mocked her, shining now blue, now green in the candle flame. "Do you command me to go?"

She said as normally as she could, "Can I order my King, sir?"

"In the Court of Love and Beauty the lady always commands."

She hesitated, groping uncertainly for words. He dropped his bantering tone.

"Truly, lady, I'll not press you. If you wish me to go I'll leave you."

She shook her head mutely and she heard him laugh softly, then he stripped off his doublet and undid his shirt at the throat. She fixed her eyes on the light golden hair on his upper chest and throat and drew back somewhat.

Recovering her courage she said, "My maid and Hugh's daughter are in the next room."

He grinned. "The walls are thick and I'll talk in whispers. If I come close, sweetheart, it will be easier."

He sank on to the bed and removed his shoes but he made no further effort to undress or alarm her. "I heard you were ill. Is it true or did you use the ruse to avoid me?"

"A little of both, sire."

He chuckled, leaning back against the pillows close by her, his hands linked behind his head.

"What I like about you is your spirit. Do you know that with the exception of Jane, I am surrounded, and ever have been, by whining women."

"I had not thought the Queen would whine, sir."

"Would you not? She costs me half a kingdom to put on her back and enrich her relations." He turned his head to watch her scandalized expression. "Nay. I'm a knave to berate her. Bessie's no virago. She's a good natured lass and I've ever had a fondness for her."

She was silent and he leaned forward towards the table. "You came not to the Hall and have eaten nothing. I brought wine and meat." As her eyes widened he nodded, "Did you not think I'd consider your needs?"

She smiled. "You are kind, sir, but I am not hungry."

"Or thirsty?"

She made no comment as he placed the wine cup in her hand and she felt the cold rim of the precious metal. He drank himself, deep, toasting her silently with a waved gesture, before his eyes caught hers over the rim of the goblet.

How had he come in so silently? Had he indeed been his own serving man, carrying the tray of cold meats she saw on the table and the wine flagon and goblets? Her cheeks burned at her own lack of foresight in leaving the bolts undrawn. She frowned. Had she not ordered Margery to secure them before going into her own room?

She sipped at the wine, watching him covertly. He did not appear drunk but there was a glitter about the eyes, a strange exhilaration she had not noted before.

"Your Grace, had you indeed dispatches for the Duchess, your mother, or did you deliberately dismiss my husband?"

"Do you love him?"

"I — I know not." Then as his brows arched upwards, "No."

"Dickon did not force the match?"

"No."

"No, he would not." He mused thoughtfully, "But he outlined the advantages of the arrangement."

"There are many." She was not in awe of him now and spoke candidly. "I had no desire to take the veil and since my father's death I had neither property nor dower."

"Poor Kate." He lifted a strand of her silky hair. "Bessie's was once your colour. It's fading." He sighed lugubriously. "We are all wilting."

She caught back a giggle and he leaned over and caught her by the shoulders. "Witch. Do you not admit your King is an old man?"

"You'd kill me if I said it."

"Aye, I would," but he shook her again.

"Do you think it?"

"That Your Grace, I have yet to find out."

He put her back against the pillows opening the bed-robe to look his fill on her slender body, pale in the shadows but glistening golden where the flickering candle caught it in dappled patches of splendour.

"I have not wanted a woman so much for a long time."

She steeled herself for the touch of his lips on her throat. Somehow his nearness brought a terrible fear. In Gloucester's presence she had felt a wild emotional confusion, with Hugh she had feared her own frigidity; with this man she was repulsed by the knowledge that if she displeased him he would destroy her as effortlessly and without feeling as she had seen him crack a walnut in his strong brown fingers. For all his geniality Edward was both selfish and calculating. All the pent up hate and desire for vengeance rose up and threatened to choke her.

Afterwards she thought it had been that which helped her to endure it. She had imagined he would be brutal, demanding; he was neither. Without a trace of embarrassment or awkwardness he stripped himself and gently withdrew her robe from her body. She lay still under his touch while his sensitive fingers fondled her breasts and thighs.

Realizing her need he waited until she was ready to surrender. Again she felt her body's delight in his skilled love-making, though her mind warned her to beware.

Hugh always slept contentedly and she imagined Edward would do so since she was sure he had been drinking heavily before he came to her bed, but he placed a masterful arm round her shoulder and drew her to him to whisper softly in her ear that they might not waken the two in the next chamber.

"You are, as I hoped, unspoilt but with a superb body, promising great depths of delight to the man who holds your heart."

She stiffened and he traced the fingers of his right hand over her cheek-bones and lips. He appeared to gain satisfaction from the beauty of textures, for she had noted that before discarding her bed-robe he had run a thumb-tip over the brocade and fur.

"You do not love Hugh?"

"My lord, I did not say I did, but how would you know — ?"

"You will never love me either. No —" he cut off her objections with a hand covering her mouth. "Do not lie. I have said I like your spirit. There is no need to flatter me. You do not love me — I don't expect that. To you I am old."

"That, sir, at least is untrue. You are a

splendid man and will ever be."

"Um," he mused. "I think you do not like me and I ask myself why. You remind me of —"

"Sir?"

"I was thinking back to my misspent youth. She was so dark, not like you at all in appearance and yet there is something. She didn't like me either, thought me feckless and selfish and vain. I am all of those things and, God, how I wanted her. She learned to love me, I think, in the end."

He lapsed into silence and she lay waiting uneasily, unwilling to speak, since he had strangely guessed at her antipathy not divining the cause and without apparent resentment.

"She was a widow, not inexperienced though I knew she had not loved her husband, yet she would not let me touch her. Poor Nell." He sighed, "I hope God accepted her in the end. All her life she feared the consequences of sin."

"But she *did* sin?"

He chuckled low in his throat. "Nay, she did not, damn her sweet eyes. I pleaded, demanded, cajoled. It was all useless and I was burning up inside. Women can be as cold as ice and torment you like the imps of hell. That was my Eleanor, cool to frigidity, until she melted in my arms after I married her."

Catherine's teeth came down on her lip, stifling her immediate reaction. He was drunk. He did not know what he said. God — if he ever recalled afterwards.

"Stillington's teeth chattered like dice in the cup. I'll always remember it, and his hand shook when he offered me the quill to sign the betrothal contract. She was calm enough and I was too hot for her to care. My lovely, virtuous Eleanor."

"She is dead, my lord?"

"Aye, dead in a nunnery where she strove to hide her sin from the world." He sighed. "She left me. It was for the best in the end. She would not have endured my treatment of her, and I could not have changed. Bess has always understood me well. She whines for possessions but never reproaches me. Eleanor would have done so repeatedly and I think I might have strangled her in my fury."

He sat up, smiling down at her. "Will *you* reproach me, Kate?"

"No, sir. Why should I do so?"

"What will you take from me, jewels, silks, land?"

She shook her head. "Already you have given me much, sir."

"Yet you *do* dislike me. Deny it if you can."

"I — am Lancastrian at heart still — perhaps." Her voice trailed off, "A traitress in your bed, sir. Beware."

"And not for the first time. Perhaps, Kate, it's how I conquer my enemies — female ones. My Bess was Lancastrian — sometimes I think she still is. I wish my male enemies were so easy to deal with."

"Fie, sir, you afeared in battle?"

"Nay, lass. That's the one occasion when I don't fear."

Her eyes widened, dark in the shadowed room. "But there must be fear of death — do you not think you might be killed?"

"Beforehand, aye. I sweat through the night in the tent, reviewing the battle plans, seeing the loopholes, the possibilities of disaster but when my squires come to arm me there's an ice-cooled head, and after, battle fever, the speed of the charge, the urge to kill and kill again —"

"And afterwards?"

"Exhilaration at victory. It's a rare delight. Some men feel drained and empty, not I. It is as if each time I begin a new life. I am born again from the fears of failure. Yet this last time in France I would not risk it. What'ere Dickon says there's more to be gained from one good treaty than ten victories. I'm getting old, I think, despite my protestations to the contrary. Tewkesbury was my last wild exultation."

"Do you not pity the slain?"

She felt him almost grope for the ability to understand and answer her.

"Aye, but there's naught to be gained from counting the cost. Men know what they risk."

"And those you condemn?"

"God knows I'm not a vengeful man but the safety of the realm is my primary concern. Rebels must die." His voice carried a note of bewilderment, as if he failed to grasp her implied reproach. "Do you not see, Kate, that if the battle had gone against me I would have gone to the block? It's kill or be killed, lass."

She leaned over and kissed him lightly. "But I am a woman and I fight with my own weapons. Do you not fear them, lord?"

He seized her and forced his mouth hard on hers till she gasped for breath and her fingers clawed at his naked shoulder.

He let her go then and laughed. "Do you concede defeat, Kate? In these engagements too, I'm usually the victor."

She rolled from him then and he pulled her back till her head arched away and the pulse beat in her exposed throat and he knew she was laughing.

She woke him early and he was quick to

rouse and realize his position.

"Your Grace, if you wish to leave me one shred of reputation, I ask that you go now."

He nodded and dressed quickly.

"I may come again? Hugh will be gone for days."

"I think you will not wish to honour me a second time."

He kissed her forehead lightly. "You do not know your own strength, Kate. It's a poor trait in the enemy. You leave me a challenge. By God, you shall like me at least. Let me try one more engagement."

Her head was turned to the neighbouring room where Margery stirred on her pallet.

"I'll go, never fear. We will talk and love again. Promise."

He pressed his lips against her fingers and she did not seek to withdraw them.

"Give me leave, Kate."

"Aye, sir, I will — but swear you will do naught to arouse my stepdaughter's suspicions."

He checked. "God's teeth, I had not thought. Very well, Kate. I'll come later today with gifts for the child —"

He withdrew the inner bolt carefully and she thought, ruefully, he had had much practice.

"Hide the wine flagon and platter in the

chest. I'll deal with them."

She rose and re-donned her bed-robe, placed the evidence of their nightly feast away from prying eyes and threw open the casement to let air into the room. The first chill of the dawn struck her and she shivered. Until this second she had been hot with anger and shame but with the cold came reaction and she went back to the crumpled bed, drew the sheet over her and cowered there, her thoughts in turmoil until Margery would come to rouse her.

CHAPTER X

Catherine eased her buttocks from the leathern covered seat of the carriage cursing inwardly the determination that had made the Queen's other ladies insist on travelling from Westminster to Baynard's Castle by road. It would have been more comfortable by river but the weather had been threatening and the covered carriage was decided upon. It had jolted and bounced her half out of her mind, and the noise of the iron wheels on the hard rutted roads seemed insupportable and even worse now they were entering upon the cobbles of the city.

The Court had returned from Windsor only two days ago and the Queen, anxious to win the Duchess of York's approval, had sent on messages of good-will and a chest of materials and two gold candlesticks for the Abbey at Berkhampstead. The silk was to be made into altar cloths and Catherine and her two chaperons were to confer with the Duchess on the most acceptable design for its embroidery.

Throughout the journey her companions had discussed at length how formidable the old lady could be.

"You know, Catherine," said Mistress Ann Greenhill, "she did not once attend court or speak one word to the Queen's Grace until the christening of the Lady Elizabeth."

Catherine thought there must be some reason for the Queen's anxiety now to secure the pacification of the Duchess. The recent months when the Duke of Clarence had stormed accusations at the Woodvilles, or sat sulkily silent at the Council Board, his arms folded on the table, had been difficult to endure and she felt the necessity for the family to close ranks to withstand any further onslaughts from the King's brother. The Queen never expended energy unless it was needful.

On his return to Windsor from Berkhampstead Hugh sought no occasion to reproach his wife. Only once more after the night of his departure had the King opportunity to come to her bed, but he continued to favour her openly, singling her out during the dancing and placing her among the Queen's ladies. Urbanely he had declared that since she had been his ward for six years and he had had no opportunity to become acquainted with her, naught now should stand in his way. Catherine knew well enough that his other dependants received not a fraction of the interest Edward showed in her, and that she was the one new subject of gossip throughout the Court. One splendid gift he made her, and that in the presence of Hugh, who bowed his gratitude, a single pear-shaped pearl on a long golden chain.

"My marriage gift," he said smoothly and called her to him to place the costly thing round her throat, stooping to kiss her heartily.

She puzzled her brain to know in what way she pleased him. Though she had responded to his ardour she knew she was a novice in the art of love, but he liked to spar with her verbally and she was forced to the conclusion that it was indeed her candid forthrightness which attracted him. He could not bear to be berated for neglect, nor did he care for giggling, insipid innocents. She was young, vital, and keen witted. He teased her about her religious life at Gupshill, but finding her ill-at-ease at such doubtful quips, he respected her sincerity and turned to other matters.

The stench rose now from the open kennels which ran through the centre of the narrow streets. Apprentices called shrilly from the open fronts of their shops and the carriage was forced to give place to mounted men-at-arms, priests on ambling palfreys and the gravely, though richly clad, merchants talking incessantly of their business affairs as they moved from guild to workshops. Now she could see the tall masts of ships anchored near the river wharves between the roofs of houses. The stink of the Thames mud at low tide mingled with the nauseous city smells and the ladies wrinkled their noses in disgust.

The driver half-turned. "We are in Thames Street, My Lady," as one grumbled, exhorting him to greater speed. "I was forced to take this round-a-bout route, since a haywain blocked our passage. We shall not be long now."

Catherine leaned forward to watch the men-at-arms ahead of them, part of their escort, jostle a group of urchins out of their way, then the captain beckoned to their driver to proceed. One of the lads screamed some abuse and as the officer lifted his arm in a threatening gesture, the rest scattered. A pieman passing gave a loud curse as the leading boy stumbled backwards and he had all he could do to recover himself and prevent his tray of fresh baked eel pies from overturning into the kennel. The urchin scrambled up again, now thoroughly alarmed, as he saw retribution threatening from the captain who angrily wheeled his horse in pursuit.

From the gate of a nearby large house a small boy emerged mounted on a pony, its bridle led by a mounted groom who accompanied him.

The urchins were frightened and ran wildly, some to one end of the street, others almost falling beneath the carriage in their efforts to escape. The carriage horses whinnied and trampled restlessly, disturbed by the confusion, and the driver pulled hard on the reins.

The boy stared round him as if terrified by the chaos in the street. He said something to the man who was with him and tried to back his pony again into the gateway. The groom shook his head, obviously encouraging him to proceed. In a panic the boy snatched at his reins and the pony, thoroughly roused now, started forward and found itself faced by the plunging carriage horses. The boy clutched at its mane wildly. Catherine could see the groom bellowing instructions, but he either could not hear or was too frightened to understand. Before the groom could ride up he had toppled from the animal's back and under the carriage.

Catherine shouted to the driver who was still struggling to hold in his lead animals. Lifting her skirts Catherine jumped from the vehicle and reached the lad at the same moment as their officer.

"Is he hurt?"

"I think one of the horses caught him on the temple with its hoofs in backing. He's unconscious."

"Poor little fellow, he was terrified. I think he has not been mounted many times before."

The groom had dismounted and joined them, kneeling on the cobbles, his face white with fear.

"Is he dead? By the Cross, My Lord of Clarence will have me hanged at Tyburn."

The captain checked. "Is this the Duke of Clarence's boy?"

"Aye, sir. He is not a good rider. My Lord has been angered by his slow progress and I thought to make him face the noise of the city. Tell me he lives."

Catherine had stooped to examine the captain's burden. "Of course he lives, man. Do not be foolish. Go, fetch a physician and instruct us where to convey him."

The captain moved to the gateway. "This is Coldharbour, Mistress Kingsford, the Duke of Clarence's town house. The boy lives here. I'll carry him in."

The child moaned. Catherine halted the captain. "He's coming round. He is not badly hurt."

The boy's large blue eyes opened and rolled as if trying to discover where he was. He struggled in the captain's arms, beating upward as if to free himself.

"Gently, gently now," Catherine soothed, "we are here to help you. You are in good hands. You fell from your pony. Your groom is here."

"No, no —" the boy almost threw himself violently to the ground. "Do not make me — please — please."

"He is shocked," Catherine said, "carry him in quickly, sir, let us get him from this noise."

The child clutched at her hand as she soothed back his thick fair hair. "There is nothing to fear. I will go with you."

Over her shoulder she called to Anne Greenhill. "You proceed with the escort. Excuse me to her Grace, the Duchess. The captain will follow in a few moments."

The captain barked his orders. "Clear the streets. Get that carriage to Baynard's Castle. It will be as well to inform the Duchess of her grandson's accident."

The child was crying, great tears rolling down his cheeks in a paroxysm of terror. Catherine urged the captain into the house, while the boy refused to relinquish his clasp of her fingers. It seemed in all this hubbub and argument the one person he wanted was this strange lady who had come to his help.

Attendants ushered them hurriedly to the child's nursery apartments. An elderly nurse, somewhat slatternly in appearance, came forward to receive him, but he screamed and kicked and Catherine feared he would fall into a fit.

"Put him on the bed, captain," she said crisply. "Leave him to me. When I was in the convent at Gupshill I assisted the infirmarian. I am not unused to sickness."

The captain willingly abandoned his burden while the nurse broke into a tirade of reproaches against those responsible for allowing injury to come to her charge.

Catherine silenced her authoritatively for the child was reacting wildly and needed rest.

"Leave us. Go and see that the doctor has been summoned as I ordered, send women with water and bring me some broth."

The woman was inclined to stand her ground but as Catherine's eyes flashed dangerously she backed hastily away. Catherine cradled the frightened child in her arms, gently attempting to discover what injuries he had sustained.

"Now, you are not frightened of me? What is your name?"

He stopped his crying to peer at her doubtfully.

"Your name?" she prompted.

He was slow before replying and she frowned. He would be about five, the same age as Gloucester's boy, like him almost beautiful with the Neville fair hair and wide eyes, as blue as the King's, but the child lacked intelligence. Even now he blinked as if striving to remember what she asked, but he was quieter now, though his fingers, scratched and grazed, still clutched at the bodice of her gown.

"You have a big bump on your head." She bent and kissed him lightly as he winced. "There, did that hurt? You are a big boy and you aren't crying any more. That's better."

A panting maid entered with a huge jug of hot water and towels. Catherine took charge.

"What is my lord's name?"

"Edward, madam."

"He is badly frightened but I do not think any bones are broken. He struggled too hard for that."

"He flies into terrible tempers, madam, and screams himself into fits. My Lord fears he is bewitched."

"What nonsense!" Catherine was unaware of any impertinence in dismissing his Grace of Clarence's accusations so simply. "There was a fight in the street, some silly boys, apprentices or beggar lads. He was frightened and fell from his pony. He could have been killed." She was undoing his doublet, loosening his shirt and wiping his brow, throat and hands. "He should not ride in the city until he is more experienced."

The maid threw her a frightened glance. "He is slow to learn, madam, and His Grace becomes angered. He said *he* could ride long before he was the Lord Edward's age." She was whispering as if she feared to be overheard and soundly whipped.

"Did he so? That was very clever of him, was it not, Edward?" Catherine retorted grimly. "But we are not all alike. I know another Edward, very much like you."

"Witch-hazel," she said to the hovering girl, "and keep nurse away. He seems frightened of her."

"He doesn't like her," the maid said doubtfully. "She is new in My Lord's service. He is always changing the nurses and attendants. I think she beats him. The Lady Margaret, his sister, dislikes and fears her." She scurried off for the lotion to apply to the bump on his forehead.

"Who?" he said suddenly. The word was jerked out as if he spoke rarely.

"Who?" she said puzzled, "oh, I know what you mean — that other Edward. He is your cousin, the son of your uncle, Duke Richard of Gloucester. He is a big boy too and fair like you."

"Edward?"

"Yes, his name is Edward like yours."

"Who?" he said again, then, as she shook

her head, "You?"

"I am Catherine."

"You don't live here." That was the longest sentence so far and she felt they were progressing. She was touched by his dependence and thought of the delicate but bright, passionate child whose tongue raced over itself, back at Middleham. So alike in appearance and unlike in nature — these two.

"No, I live at the palace. I am one of the Queen's ladies."

There was a knock on the door and the maid admitted the physician, tall and forbidding, in his long robe of grey gaberdine.

"Stay." The child implored her and she nodded and stood back to allow the man to approach while keeping his hot little fingers tightly grasped in hers.

Though still alarmed, at Catherine's bidding, he allowed the doctor to examine him. Promising to return immediately to his side Catherine went to the door with the man.

"Is the Duke in the house?"

"I think not."

The man pursed his lips. "There seem to be no broken bones. The bump on his head will be painful but he seems fevered and will be more so during the coming night. God preserve us from a Tertian fever or some childish ailment. The Duke is so concerned about the boy's health."

"Is he unduly delicate?"

"No, but he is easily alarmed and subject to fits of violent temper which exhaust him for days." He peered at her suspiciously. "Are you a member of the household?" His eyes passed over her fashionable attire, his manner becoming more noticeably deferential.

"I am one of the Queen's ladies. On our way to Baynard's Castle to visit the Duchess of York our carriage became involved in the accident. Since I was convent bred, I have no fear of sickness."

He looked back towards the boy's bed. "So you will not stay?"

"I should report to the Duchess and later return to Westminster before dark."

"A pity." He pulled his lip. "The boy trusts you and that is rare for him. If you could stay near him tonight it would lessen the risk of complications."

She shrugged "With the Duke's permission I am perfectly willing to do so. A message can be dispatched to Westminster."

His face cleared. "I would be more at rest in my mind. I will leave him a soothing posset but warn you, it is difficult to get him to swallow any medicine if a stubborn mood is on him."

"I'll do my best."

"Aye, he should sleep."

The little prince seemed quieter now. The ugly bump disfigured his forehead and there would be a great purple bruise later. He lay quiet watching her with those great blue eyes, while she issued her orders to his attendants.

At noon she persuaded him to take some broth. The moment his nurse entered the nursery he became agitated and firmly Catherine dismissed her. She marvelled that the household servants did not oppose her will, but her air of authority and the doctor's support lent her instructions added weight. After he had eaten, the little maid whose name, Catherine discovered, was Betsy brought her some cold meats and ale and sat near the bed while Catherine ate her own dinner.

She said hesitantly, "There is no word of My Lord."

"Have attendants been searching?"

"Yes, madam. He does not appear to be in the city. He was not at the Tower."

Catherine thought, wryly, that he was unlikely to be at Westminster Palace either.

"The little Lady Margaret would like to see her brother, madam."

Catherine glanced doubtfully at the lad who was calmer now and playing with some cord making cat's cradles on his fingers.

"She is good with him."

"I cannot refuse to admit her, but nurse —"

"I will bring her in."

Catherine nodded and Betsy disappeared and came back in moments with a small girl of about seven years of age. Her hair was darker than her brother's, but her skin had the pink and white prettiness of all the Nevilles and her blue eyes were alight and intelligent. Catherine smothered a faint sigh of relief. Another excited and difficult child would be hard to bear.

She curtsied to the child who dutifully returned her greeting.

"Your brother is not seriously hurt, lady, but the doctor says he must be kept quiet. Do you understand?"

"Yes." The child regarded her carefully. "I will play with him till he sleeps. Nurse has gone to her bed. She has given herself a headache." She smiled suddenly and with a sudden pang Catherine saw the faintest trace of resemblance to her uncle, Gloucester, the same rare charm appearing at intervals. "I think it was because she flew into such a rage."

Despite herself Catherine smiled back and the girl went to her brother who greeted her with rapture.

By evening the Duke had still not returned. The Lady Margaret went back to her nurse's charge. Edward's fever mounted. He grew hot and restless, throwing off the linen sheets and complaining of pain in his head. After much coaxing Catherine persuaded him to swallow the bitter-tasting draught the doctor had left him. She gave him marchpane as a reward and at last he settled. Since no one had sought to oust her from her position as temporary nurse she settled to rest in a chair by his side. Betsy had waited on her throughout the day and brought her more food. She peeled a pear, keeping her eyes on the hunched figure of the child.

It was still high summer and there was no need to call for candles. Moths fluttered in through the partly opened casement and Catherine rose to close it. The night air from the river would be hazardous but she thought the room would become hot and fetid and did so reluctantly.

She was drowsing comfortably when she was woken harshly by the noise of return below, the whinny and stamp of horses, boots ascending the stone stair and the strident calls of the returned master. She rose and bent anxiously over her charge. He was flushed and he stirred, but relapsed into sleep. Catherine bit her lip in perplexity. If the Duke had returned he would undoubtedly wish to see the child, satisfy himself that all was well with him, but it was a pity. If woken the young

Edward might not sleep again tonight.

Betsy had stirred uneasily. She had settled herself against the wall on a joint-stool. In the dim twilight Catherine could see the girl was visibly alarmed. So Clarence had a reputation for brutality among his servants.

The door was thrust open abruptly and a man strode in. The nurse behind him was tearfully endeavoring to explain, her hands twisted nervously in the folds of her apron.

Catherine rose and curtsied low. "My Lord," she said respectfully but warningly, "the prince sleeps. The doctor said it was inadvisable to waken him."

He was tall like the King but less burly. A riot of fair curls descended almost to his waist.

"Pish, woman, be silent," he roared at the nurse who hid her face in the apron.

His voice was thick and even in the dim light Catherine noted that he was flushed, his eyes red rimmed from heavy drinking. He came forward truculently. "Who in God's name are you?"

"Catherine Kingsford, Your Grace."

He blinked owlishly. "And who, by the Holy Rood, is Catherine Kingsford?"

"I am one of the Queen's ladies, sir. I can explain."

"One of that cursed Woodville brood in my

house and near my son?"

His voice rose to a bellow. Her eyes went to the child who woke and called out.

"My Lord, let us leave the sick room —"

"They tell me he fell from his pony."

"He did so, sir, but is not badly hurt. He was frightened."

The Duke strode to the bed where the child, now fully roused, cowered back, clutching the silken covering round him.

"Frightened? The boy's lily-livered. What cause had he to be frightened? The pony's quiet enough. God's teeth, have I reared a coward from Warwick's stock?"

Edward wailed shrilly and Catherine, angered, swept by the Duke and caught him to her.

"My Lord," she said imperiously, "now is not the time to discuss the matter. The Lord Edward must rest."

The Duke's blue eyes, slightly protuberant, blazed with drunken fury.

"Will you tell me how to handle my own brat? The lad's besotted. He's no Plantagenet, sure, sometimes I wonder if his mother foisted some low-bred archer's child on me — or else the cursed sorcery of that palace witch has worked on his wits."

There was a shocked gasp from the group of attendants, hovering in the corridor beyond the door. Catherine's face whitened with anger.

"My Lord, in your child's interest I request you to leave his chamber and let me calm him. He trusts me."

He raised his arm threateningly. "Why in God's name should he trust you, get out of my house, back to the Woodville witch you serve." He was beside himself, the bellow changed to a querulous squeal.

"If you strike me, Your Grace," she said evenly, "I shall assuredly strike you back. Think what a crass fool you would look in open court accusing a commoner of striking a royal personage, because he was in a drunken rage. I should die, undoubtedly, but I would speak out in my own defence."

There was a stunned silence. Clarence lurched unsteady on his feet. Still she thought he would either attack her or break a blood vessel in his fury. Edward sobbed passionately and abruptly she turned from the Duke, lifted the frightened child in her arms and, going to a chair, seated herself, cradling him to her heart.

"Get out." The Duke waved an impatient hand, "All of you except Giles. Come here, lad, and help me to my chamber." His smouldering gaze swept over Catherine who ignored him, her head bent over the child, then on to the maid who backed hastily from him. He gave a blasphemous oath and staggered out of the room with the help of a squire.

Catherine sat on rocking the sick child till his frenzied sobs quietened to little moans and whimpers, then she rose and returned him to his bed.

"Betsy," she said softly, "close the door and go back to your stool. I think the Lord Edward will sleep again now."

CHAPTER XI

"Madam."

Catherine's head jerked as she felt the gentle shake on her shoulder. She opened her eyes to find Betsy smiling down at her. The maid had slept throughout the night while she had remained wakeful. Then after the Lord Edward had taken breakfast and fallen off to sleep again she had herself curled up in a chair and allowed her eyes to close, worn out by the stresses and strains of the previous night. She had known Betsy would take her turn guarding the boy.

"Madam, the Duchess is here. She has asked to see you."

"The Duchess?" Catherine struggled up, somewhat alarmed.

"Her Grace the Duchess of York. She sent last night to enquire after the Lord Edward's health. She is waiting in the parlour."

"But the Duke?" Catherine said desperately. "Has His Grace not gone himself to greet his mother?"

Betsy's pleasant, homely face fell. "He —

he cannot be roused, madam," she said uncertainly.

Catherine snorted her indignation. So His Grace was in a drunken stupor, snoring in his chamber and his attendants too afraid of his fury to waken him — so much for his concern about his son.

"Bring me some water and a comb, child," she said hurriedly, "and while I am gone, stay with the Lord Edward."

Last night she had removed her hennin, since it was cumbersome and weighty. Her hair was now dishevelled, strands falling about her shoulders. She freshened herself and Betsy assisted her to pin up her hair and rearrange her hennin. She shook out the ample folds of her gold and brown brocaded gown, now sadly crumpled, and having done her best to put to rights her appearance, descended to the parlour.

Cecily, Duchess of York, sat stiffly alone in the arm-chair near the window. She was clothed from head to foot in unrelieved mourning which she had not put off since the news reached her that her husband, Duke Richard, and her second son, Edmund, Duke of Rutland, had been slain after Wakefield. Her coif was nun-like, but the morning sun streamed through the window on to her proud, ascetic countenance. She was still a beautiful stately woman. Proud Cecily they called her, and Catherine could believe the stories of all those who had stood in awe of her. She sank into a deep curtsy until bidden to rise.

"Sit down, Mistress Kingsford." The Duchess graciously waved her to a chair opposite. "You must be over-wearied. How is little Edward?"

"He is better, Your Grace, but still a little flushed, so I gave him another draught to help him rest. He has eaten."

"I hear there are no bones broken."

"The physician says not, Your Grace."

"Good. And my son, the Duke? You have informed him of Edward's progress?"

Catherine hesitated. "He returned to Coldharbour late, Your Grace. I think —"

"He is dead drunk?"

Catherine flushed to the roots of her hair at the Duchess's cold statement of fact.

"Oh, don't quibble, Mistress Kingsford. These days he is seldom anything else." She inclined her head slightly to examine Catherine's features. Again she flushed under the Duchess's scrutiny.

"You are very lovely. Are you my son's mistress?"

Catherine's lips parted soundlessly. She stared at the Duchess stupefied and thanked

God and the Virgin they were alone together. "Your son?" she echoed, a trifle foolishly.

"I hardly think even George would have the effrontery to seduce his sick child's nurse in the sickroom, and certainly I was not referring to Dickon. I ask you, madam, if you are the King's mistress?"

Catherine looked down at her hands loosely clasped on her knee.

"The King has honoured me, Your Grace," she said quietly. "I have become no one's kept mistress."

"H'm." The Duchess continued to eye her suspiciously. "I have heard some such talk. You look demure enough but I admire your honesty. Do you love him?"

Catherine gasped. "No, Your Grace." The members of this family were shameless. Had not the Kind asked her the self-same question of her relationship with Hugh?

"Since you do not appear to see yourself in the role of the King's mistress, what then, do you expect from him? Land, jewels? I would not imagine so from what I see of you already, on such short acquaintance."

Catherine was evasive for once. "His Grace the King is hard to resist, madam."

"Well," she said shortly, "he has never been known to force a maid." She gave a little laugh. "He has never had cause to do so. They fall into his arms like ripe plums from the orchard tree."

There was a silence and Catherine felt impelled to break it. "Your Grace, I regret I did not come to Baynard's Castle as I was bidden by the Queen. I must tender my humble apologies but —"

"Tush, girl, it's clear you had something more pressing to claim your attention. Let us visit my grandson and then you will return with me to Baynard's Castle for the rest of today and tonight. I will send you to Westminster in the morning."

"Your Grace, I should not leave the prince."

The Duchess had risen, now she turned and regarded Catherine piercingly with her faded blue eyes.

"It is impossible that you remain here."

"But —"

"Do you not see how it would anger Edward if you remain under Clarence's roof? I can hardly imagine that it will please your husband either."

Catherine bit her lip, curtsied and stood aside for the Duchess to precede her to the nursery. As they ascended the stair she told the other woman quietly of her opinion regarding the children's nurse.

"I am not surprised at this state of affairs. After the disgraceful business over Ankaret

Cogges, he will trust no one with the children, changing their attendants almost as often as he discards his underclothing. It will not do. Young Edward is nervous and backward. He needs special care."

"I think the maid, Betsy, would be good with him. She seems a trustworthy girl and in no wise flighty."

"Very well then, I shall place the boy in her charge."

"But the Duke?"

The Duchess smiled faintly. "I will handle the Duke." Edward had woken but was still drowsy. He did not seem so much in awe of his haughty grandmother as one might have supposed, but it was clear that Betsy walked in fear and trembling in her presence.

Since the physician was expected and the child obviously greatly improved the Duchess gave her orders succinctly, placing Betsy in charge, leaving a message for her son to present himself at Baynard's Castle as soon as convenient and took her leave, Catherine in tow.

As she took her seat in the Duchess's barge she was grateful to have been spared a second encounter with My Lord of Clarence.

It was with some embarrassment that Catherine presented herself in the Queen's apartment at Westminster the following day, but the Queen expressed regret at the accident to the Lord Edward and her satisfaction that Catherine's errand was completed, the design for the altar-cloth selected and the work put in hand.

"My dear, you must be wearied after your adventure," she said genially. "Please allow yourself as long as you wish to rest before presenting yourself for duties in attendance."

Gratefully Catherine accepted her dismissal and went at once to her own small apartment at the rear of the palace. She was anxious about Hugh's reaction. Recently she had seen little of him and had slept by his side on only two occasions since their journey South. The King had occupied Kingsford's attention on matters of his own and the Queen, having recently sent her to Baynard's Castle, they found themselves either by accident or design repeatedly apart. She had not been sorry, her embarrassment of guilt, and Hugh's complacent acceptance of it, making her acutely uncomfortable in his presence. They found it difficult to know how to address each other and Catherine had found herself grateful for the addition of Cecily to their company, as serious talk was perforce denied them. Surely soon, the King would send Hugh north again to Middleham and she wondered what pattern her future would take. She had expected to live quietly on her own manor-lands at Newburgh with the children, while Hugh was in attendance on Gloucester, but she saw plainly that if the King expressed a desire for her to remain at Westminster she would be powerless to object.

She was met by Cecily, surprisingly in a torrent of tears. The child had seemed so much happier since leaving Leicestershire that Catherine was astonished.

"Cecily, what is it?"

"It's Janet. Messages came for our father that she is seriously ill and he left at once for Cadeby. Oh, Catherine, if she should die. She is so little."

Catherine looked across Cecily's dark head to Margery Whittacker, in whose charge she had left the girl.

"Some minor childish ailment, Mistress. I have told Mistress Cecily that Janet will soon be well and Sir Hugh back at Court."

"Poor Hugh. He must be concerned and I not by him."

"The King granted him leave."

Catherine nodded, smoothing Cecily's hair back from her brow. "Now you must smile. I hope you did not worry your father so. He has enough problems."

Cecily once over her initial confidence, dried her tears and went off with Margery back to her embroidery while Catherine rested. She felt increasing guilt at her treatment of Hugh, yet at the back of her mind she felt a nagging sense of relief that for some time at least she would not have to face his reproachful gaze.

On the fourth day after her return a messenger wearing the livery of the Clarence Bull was brought into her presence, where she sat among the Queen's ladies, laughing at some sallies of the dandified young Tom Grey, Marquess of Dorset. Puzzled she took the letter he offered her, waiting respectfully for her to acquaint herself of its contents and give him an answer.

It was short but respectful. His Grace of Clarence requested that Mistress Kingsford would visit Coldharbour since the Lord Edward fretted for her and his progress was set back. If she would do so with the Queen's permission she would win the Duke's gratitude.

Excusing herself, while Dorset peered after her and the messenger thoughtfully, she sought the Queen. The King lounged in the parlour for once enjoying the company of his family. It was a pleasant, domestic scene, the Lady Elizabeth leaning across the back of her father's chair obviously wheedling him into purchasing for her some new trinket, the younger boy, Prince Richard, on a footstool near his mother's chair reading aloud his lesson.

Catherine curtsied and explained the Duke of Clarence's request.

Edward's eyebrows rose. "Go, certainly. I will provide you with an escort. You will need a woman, since, I imagine you will leave Cecily in your maid's care. Tell George I wish to be kept informed of the lad's condition."

Prince Richard's bright eyes sparkled. "Poor Edward. Tell him when he is well he must come to Westminster and play with me since my Edward is now off to Ludlow."

"I will, little Prince."

The King rose and moved to a carved chest, lifted the lid and searched about inside.

"Ah, a beastiary newly come from Master Caxton's press. Will you take it as my gift to my nephew?"

Catherine's face lit up. "Oh, Your Grace, it will delight him. He loves animals." She turned the pages with pleasure. "And these pictures are beautiful. Edward of Gloucester has such a book and it is never far from his hand."

The King's expression was grave. "If it will help him progress in his learning, I shall be more than satisfied. I worry about the lad."

She curtsied and withdrew, leaving with

Clarence's messenger, since the man told her the Duke had provided a waiting woman to serve her.

"She is in the Duke's barge by the King's steps," he assured her.

On arrival at Coldharbour she was taken at once to the Lord Edward. He greeted her rapturously, throwing his arms round her neck and hugging her tightly. She experienced a warm glow of joy. Cecily was not demonstrative, though they were happy in each other's company, and since she had been the only child of her parents she had not known the affection of younger children. It seemed that the young Edward sensed in her a rock-like strength to which he could cling, when all round him seemed to shift dangerously.

He was delighted with the book and turned the pages with extreme care, pointing to the animals as Catherine named them for him. Betsy said that he was better but each night became flushed and restless.

"It is so difficult to get him to sleep," she explained. "There is always noise below when the Duke entertains his lordly companions but the Lord Edward seems afraid when he hears their arrivals and their loud laughter."

Privately Catherine wondered if the night's revelry often brought the Duke to the boy's chamber, his eyes glazed with drinking and at such times, he lashed him with his tongue, as he had before, or levelled accusations the child had no way of answering or understanding.

An attendant knocked on the door and Betsy admitted him.

"The Duke is in the parlour and would have speech with you, Mistress Kingsford."

Catherine rose from her stool near Edward's bed somewhat apprehensively, nodded to Betsy and accompanied the man.

Clarence rose at her entry and she proffered him her deepest curtsy, recalling with shame, her insolence at their last meeting. He kissed her finger-tips and bade her rise.

"Mistress Kingsford," he said gravely, and now that it was not thickened with wine fumes, his voice, though higher than Gloucester's, was as pleasant and resonant as those of his brothers, "I think I greeted you on the last occasion of our meeting with less than the respect and gratitude I owed you."

She checked as he drew her to a chair near to his own. "Your Grace — I fear —"

"Please," he smiled, and it lit up his whole face, "do not let us dwell on it, for I would have your goodwill, for my son's sake."

He was still in mourning, but his gold chain set with uncut rubies and emeralds sparked with hot fire from the sun and the jewels smouldered. Now she saw that he was perfectly sober today and as fine a man as the King, indeed had his face not still borne the marks of recent debauchery he would have been undoubtedly the most handsome of the Plantagenet brothers. He was tall but without Edward's weight and had the same vivid colouring, the complexion fair though somewhat florid, and the wealth of thick, almost red-gold hair, which he wore longer than the King curling on to his shoulders. There were traces of arrogance in the flaring nostrils of his high bridged nose and his blue eyes were heavy-lidded and the flesh beneath puffed and swollen. His mouth was as beautiful as any woman's but it betrayed weakness of character in its querulous downward droop. She could see little resemblance to Gloucester, who assuredly rather featured his father, York, than Clarence and the King.

"The Lord Edward is better," she said hesitantly. "The King was concerned for him and I took him a book as a gift."

"Was he?" The mouth hardened as if his brother's concern for his nephew displeased him.

Catherine blinked anxiously. "He asked me to take back a report of his progress and to convey to you his sympathy. Prince Richard expressed a desire for his cousin's company. He seems such a lively, charming child that —"

"I would never allow my child to enter a household dominated by the Woodvilles." He smiled at her dismay. "You see, I remain staunch in my dislike of my brother's wife and rely on your good sense to keep your own counsel concerning my rash words."

"My Lord —"

Again he smiled and she marvelled at the brilliance of his personal charm when he chose to use it.

"I cannot believe that the woman who staunchly declared her intention of striking me would lack the courage of honesty. I think you know opinions, Mistress. They have been aired too well in public for them to escape your notice."

She dropped polite fencing. "I do, My Lord, but I also think you mistaken. I cannot willingly believe the King would harbour evil intent towards your children."

The heavy lids swept back and his blue eyes regarded her piercingly. "You may be right, but he is not the only one I fear at Westminster." He dropped his serious note and said smiling, "Will you dine with me alone or do you fear I might strike you? If so, I will call a lady." He extended his hands towards her. "See, not a shake. I am recovered, lady."

She laughed. "I would be honoured, sir."

He was excellent company. They talked mainly of the children. She found it hard to remember that this was the man who had falsely betrayed her father, threatened the safety of Gloucester's Anne, and raved like a madman against his brother's rights. Were there two separate entities behind that engaging personality? What made this man so vascillating, first supporting his brother, then turning traitor and marrying Warwick's daughter in the teeth of Edward's opposition? Then again he had turned volte-face at Barnet and abandoned Warwick to his death. She was bewildered. She could not think he was a fool. His sallies were as witty as Dorset's or Rivers's. Did his weakness for the wine cup turn him from a man to a sot? If so, there was some underlying cause. Selfish he might be, but she did not sense the same cruelty as there was in Edward, nor the fanatical loyalty to a cause that might make Richard relentless in punishment. Clarence would bend with the wind, she might feel contempt but not hatred for him.

"You will come again?" He pleaded with the sincerity of a youth. "Edward loves you, and I have such pleasure in your company, that I would wish such an opportunity to repeat itself soon."

"You honour me, Your Grace."

"Catherine." He took her hand and held it tight. "I would have your friendship, not your flattery."

"It is yours, sir."

He hesitated. "Have you Edward's favour?"

"He has been to my bed. I am not his mistress in the proper sense of the term."

"Do you love him?" She wondered how many times she must answer this pertinent question.

"No, sir, but I rejoice in his favour."

"And your husband?"

"I respect him, he is a good man, but almost a stranger to me."

He gave a little sigh of content. "Thank you for giving me your confidence."

He called his attendant to accompany her up river and himself escorted her to the quay steps.

CHAPTER XII

Catherine was seated at the table, completing her toilet when Hugh strode into their apartment.

He looked wearied and strained but did not bear the terrible desolation of bereavement and she was relieved to know that Janet still lived.

He sank down on a chair and dismissed Margery who was dressing her hair.

"She is recovering but they were forced to bleed her and she is weak," he said grimly as he removed his riding boots.

"Thank God and the Virgin," she said fervently. "You thought it safe enough to leave her?"

"Aye, she does well enough. I am not my own man these days and the King commands my duty."

She dropped her eyes to her jewel box. She read dejection in the set of his shoulders and pitied his loneliness. The man despaired. He wanted her and all the court knew she had been Edward's light of love. Had she not done him enough harm? He made no effort to embrace her but called for his squire to arrange for him to bathe.

"Do you dine in Hall?" she said hastily. "Would it not be wiser to rest?"

He eyed her coldly. "Aye, madam," he said, "but I refer to bask in the reflected glory of my wife's popularity."

It was the nearest he had come to censuring her and she turned back to her mirror. Assuredly he had had leisure during these last days of journeying to think about their relationship and its barren nature.

She had been twice to Coldharbour. On each occasion Clarence had treated her with grave courtesy. She had bitten her lip in the barge on her return this last time. He had not spoken of love, but he would do so. She had come to recognize his innate loneliness. He was surrounded by friends who flattered and fawned on him. He could trust not one of them, and, like his son's, his was a nature that needed a rock on which to lean.

The Duchess of York, clearly, had little love to give him. She had been openly contemptuous. Had he been over-dominated by mother, elder brother, his cousin Warwick? Now that Warwick was gone did he lack guidance, direction? They had all used him and discarded him. Now, guiltily, she realized he was open to her influence. Her weapons were clearly defined. If she had the will she could destroy him and with him the King's peace.

Catherine found herself the subject of many veiled glances as she took her place at table with her husband and later she noted how conversation died as he drew her towards a group of chattering courtiers.

Their glances were partly directed at her, partly at a woman seated alone, some feet away from the King's chair. She was older than Catherine, not nearly so stately of form, but when near enough, Catherine saw that her features were comely and her eyes merry. She was dressed without affectation, though richly, and she wore a fortune in emeralds at her throat.

She heard the whispers. "Shore's wife is back then. She seems recovered. So it was not the pox or she would have been disfigured."

So this was Jane Shore, the merchant's wife, the King's merry mistress. She bore herself well and without flaunting audacity which Catherine knew would have sorely irked the Queen. As usual, tonight, she seemed in no way disturbed by the reappearance of Edward's favourite. Catherine noted with some surprise that two other pairs of eyes surveyed the noted beauty with some care, those of

Thomas Grey, Marquess of Dorset, and the older ones of the King's Chamberlain, Lord Hastings.

The King drank deep and danced little. He partnered his eldest daughter, the Queen as always declined to take her place on the floor and at length he turned to Mistress Shore.

As they moved together in the pattern of the dance Catherine heard his hearty laugh ring through the hall and when he returned her to her chair, his hand lingered on hers.

When she was summoned to the King's side Catherine was faintly surprised. She had thought herself eclipsed tonight, but he took her hand and led her into the dance.

"And how is young Edward? We hear you are constantly at Coldharbour these days?"

His tone was chill and she flushed to the roots of her hair.

"He does well, Your Grace. He likes my company."

"And my brother? How is His Grace of Clarence, in good health and spirits, I hope?"

So the King's spies had reported Clarence's interest in her.

"He appears well, sir."

"Now the boy is recovered you will not need to journey to the city so often. The weather will soon become inclement. The river can prove treacherous."

He was warning her to avoid the Duke's town house. She was piqued. Was she the King's property? Had he bought her with a single jewel and the attentions he had paid her in public?

She said coolly, "I am honoured to have been favoured by the interest of three royal brothers, sire."

"Three?" He snapped the word at her irritably.

"His Grace of Gloucester was kind enough to arrange my marriage," she said evenly.

His mouth tightened and those blue eyes glittered as they had that night in the candle flame. She felt a little prickle of fear down the length of her spine, then he was smiling again, though his eyes remained hard.

When he returned her to Hugh, he said, "I am glad your daughter is better, Sir Hugh, for you have recently been forced to neglect your wife, my ward. When she goes again to the city, I wish her to be under your protection."

Hugh bowed as the King moved away to the merry gaze of Mistress Shore.

Catherine's face flamed and she inclined her head stiffly as several people passed and saluted them. How dare the King order her husband to keep a leash on her as though she were some unruly hound bitch.

"I wish to leave the Hall," she said through gritted teeth.

Hugh's fingers pressed harshly on hers. "You will do nothing of the kind. We have not been dismissed and you will remain and learn to bear your humiliation with dignity."

Tears pricked at her eyes as she stood rigidly by her husband's side until the King and the intimate members of his household left the hall.

Once in their chamber he waited until Margery had assisted her to undress and wrapped her in her bed-robe. From behind the bed-curtains she heard him undress and dismiss his squire. She seated herself at her mirror and indicated to Margery that she wished her to brush her hair.

He came behind her.

"You may go, Margery."

Margery curtsied and withdrew. Catherine quivered with anger. She snatched up the brush and began to sweep it with some force down the long lengths of her hair. He caught her hand and stilled it.

"That will do. There are things to be discussed."

She swung round to him, her chin jutting obstinately. "Oh?"

"The talk in the hall was of you, tonight, mistress, and your escapades into the city."

"I thought it was of Mistress Shore."

"She does not concern us."

"She concerns the King."

His dark eyes narrowed. "The King is angered. You heard what he said. You are to go no more to His Grace of Clarence's house."

Her lip curled. "The King is to turn his favour from me and back to Mistress Shore but I am not to amuse myself."

He struck her sharply. "Slut."

She was so startled and though the blow carried no weight behind it, was taken by surprise by the suddenness of his action so much so that she bumped her head against the Venetian travelling mirror. She recovered quickly and faced him proudly, her hand against her smarting cheek.

"What angers you, Hugh, that I have acted the slut with the King or that his favours have turned from me? What will you lose — a barony? Had you expected to gain more than when you betrayed my father?"

He jerked her to her feet, his hands biting into the soft flesh of her shoulders. Blindly she sought to avert her face, fearing a second, smashing follow-up blow for she saw now that she had roused him. His dark face was crimson with fury and his lips curled back in a snarl.

"Do you dare taunt me with my own restraint?" Then, as her attack dawned upon him, he shook her hard. "What put such idiocy into your head?"

She was not afraid and in no mood for conciliation. "My father died because he was believed to be Sir William Newberry. You did not undeceive his judges. You identified him as the traitor and you gained his land."

He let her fall back on to the chair so that her neck jerked with a snap and she felt it tenderly. He leaned across her and she saw that the angry flush had died from his cheeks. He was deadly pale.

"Your father was executed for fighting against his King. No one betrayed him. He brought his own death about by his own crass folly in choosing the losing side, the fortunes of war, my child."

"Thousands of Lancastrians walked from the field with the King's pardon," she blazed back at him. "He forgave all freely, save those who plotted with Warwick against him secretly. My father had never left our manor until Tewkesbury. He was mistaken for his cousin, Newberry of Lulworth. That's why he died and that is why you inherited Newburgh."

He seemed stunned by what she said. His brows drew together in puzzlement.

"I don't understand."

"You *do* understand, well enough. Did you not tell Gloucester he was indeed Newberry of Lulworth?"

"As God is my judge, I did not, nor did I know of any such misunderstanding."

"You saw him die."

"I saw many die. I knew neither your father nor William Newberry by sight. I gave no evidence at that trial nor was any asked of me. Your father pleaded guilty to the charge of treason. I regretted the necessity but I was helpless to intervene."

He turned from her, a hand across his brow. "God's wounds, you married me, charging me in your heart with such a sin?"

She was silent and he swung round again. "Answer me. Do you not believe what I say?"

She gave a tight little shrug. "What does it matter? The result was the same. I have found that in your world, brother betrays brother without qualm. Why should I think you less venal than the next?"

He moved from her and sank on to the bed, his face in his hands.

"You lay beside me with that in your heart?"

She made no answer and he looked up at her challengingly.

"Why did you wed me, Catherine?"

"I told you. Gloucester wished the match

and it seemed necessary."

"If you wanted to hurt me you found a way. I love you, Catherine."

There was no answer and she turned from him, picked up the brush and continued with her task.

He said quietly, "I shall seek the King's leave to go North, tomorrow." Her hand paused, then continued smoothly. "I shall establish you in Leicestershire with the children. I'll not trouble you. I shall go straightway to Middleham."

"No," she said briefly.

"What do you mean?"

"It does not please me to bury myself in Leicestershire. I shall petition the Queen to remain in her service."

He was defeated and he knew it. Her final word was doubly venomed.

"Seek to take Cecily from me and you'll rue it. She has affection for me and will choose to stay. What love have you ever given her? Your attention has ever been to pleasing those above you and acquiring more land."

She did not turn when the door slammed on his departing figure. She picked up an ivory comb to deal with a tangle of hair. She tugged until the tears sprang from her eyes and its slender handle snapped in her fingers. She flung it down and threw herself on to the bed, burying her head in the pillow and beating her fist against it impotently, while she sobbed out her grief and anger.

Exhausted at last she turned on her back and lay staring up at the ceiling.

CHAPTER XIII

Catherine was soon to discover that the King's orders concerning her were to be strictly kept, Hugh now constituting himself her jailer, either on his own account or in his anxiety not to anger Edward further. He stayed grimly by her side when she rode out hawking or hunting with the Court party and only left her side in the palace if the King included her in his circle of intimates after the feasting in the Hall.

Indeed Edward had apparently soon forgotten his ill-humour over the affair of Clarence and favoured her as much as ever, though these nights were spent with Mistress Shore or the Queen, since he did not come again to Catherine's bed. He need not have troubled himself about Hugh, since he too had deserted her chamber. She did not know where he slept or with whom and she cared less. He made no effort to leave Westminster and she imagined the King had withheld his consent.

Now, more than ever, she was determined to communicate with the Duke of Clarence. It was insufferable that she should be treated as a prisoner without the right to meet, in private, whomsoever she wished.

But how? The Lord Edward was fully recovered and no excuse lay in that direction. Clarence never came to the palace. His absence at his brother's court was noted and became the subject of interest in the French Ambassador's report to his master, King Louis.

There was one way only of contacting Clarence and that was through the young Edward. Catherine cudgelled her brains to think of some means.

She called Cecily to her one day towards the end of August.

"I want you to go with Margery to the Duke of Clarence's house in Thames Street and visit the Lord Edward for me. Take him my gift of these sweetmeats. He will ask after me but he will be glad to see you and possibly you may meet the Lady Margaret who is a delightful child. This embroidered handkerchief in its own little box is for her." She turned to Hugh who stood scowling, waiting for her to hasten since they were to attend the Queen on a leisurely hawking party.

"You have no objection, sir, have you? The child will miss me and you have said you do not wish me to go."

He nodded briefly. "There can be no harm for Cecily to go in your place provided she is under Margery's care."

Cecily was delighted at the thought of the row down river and chattered away with Margery.

Hugh accompanied the King to the Tower the next morning. The Council would meet later and the King's escort would wait dutifully some hours. Catherine dressed soberly and with care, called a groom she could trust, and rode into the city. In the Chepe she dismounted and bade the man wait while she passed into the goldsmith's shop.

She was greeted with deference since she was obviously from the Court. She took from its velvet covered box, Edward's marriage gift on its fine, long chain.

"The clasp is faulty," she said as she gave it to the senior craftsman. "It is the King's gift. I must wear it tonight. Can it be repaired?"

"Certainly, mistress —"

"Have you some private place out of the sun —"

The man bowed. "The solar is kept clear for customers who wish to examine gems in comfort."

She smiled. "Show me some seal rings. I would like to purchase one for my husband."

The solar was dark and stuffy but well furnished and private. The noise from the street penetrated only faintly through the tightly closed casements. Catherine longed to fling them wide but feared to let in the foul odours from the kennels, blocked now with refuse, since it had not rained for days, nor had she the desire to hear the strident calls of the apprentices lads "What do you lack?" or the bawdy bandinage of the house-wives who leaned from the windows of the overhanging upper storeys to gossip with their neighbours across the street. She sat down to wait patiently and at last her patience was rewarded when the craftsman escorted George of Clarence into the room and placed a selection of gem stones for his perusal, and, bowing, withdrew.

"My Lord, you received my note?"

"Margaret gave it to me. It was in the box."

"My husband watches me closely. I wished to explain. The King is angered by your interest and I have been forbidden to come again to Coldharbour. It is kind of you to wait upon me here. I realize —"

He took her hand, imprisoning it fast. "I am honoured that you asked for such a meeting. Sit, Mistress Kingsford. The man will leave us some time in private. I imagine he is faced with many such assignations." His teeth gleamed white in the shaded room. "This is a rare occurrence indeed for me and the need for caution adds extra spice to my pleasure." His mood changed and she saw him frown. "However, I'd not have you in danger."

"My husband escorts the King to the Tower. I am safe for some hours and I can trust my groom." She attempted to extricate her fingers and he loosened his clasp, thinking it gave her pain, but he still held her hand loosely.

"So Edward forbids our meeting." His voice shook with passion. "God's Blood, a fine brother, who opposes me every step of the way."

"He is jealous and has no cause."

"Has he not?" He peered up at her, his ephemeral mood once more altered. "What think you of George of Clarence? Our first meeting did not augur well. You are a woman such as I have never known, strong-willed, capable, honest. I love you, Catherine Kingsford, and I think I have never truly loved any creature so, before."

"My Lord, you must not speak so. The children —"

"Oh, aye. I have affection for them but the lad is slow-witted and they both fear me. I am a weak man, Catherine, there, I admit it. I'll face many things when not in my cups, but God knows I turn to the wine when I can no longer live with the truth about myself."

She leaned towards him and with her free hand touched his lips lightly. "Speak not so slightingly of yourself. Was it not Clarence who fought bravely at Barnet and Tewkesbury? After the King you are the greatest man in England."

"After the King." He echoed her words in a whisper and she read in the simple phrase all the pent up poison in the man's soul. "While Edward lolls in Westminster beside that which he married, he keeps me from mine own."

She looked round hastily. "Be cautious, My Lord."

But he was lost to all restraint. "Place a testament in my mother's hand and ask her to swear Edward is truly Great York's son and I tell you, Catherine, she will not imperil her mortal soul." He released her hand at last and paced the rush strewn floor of the solar. "He fears me and till that Woodville low-born wench bore him boys, I was the heir of England."

Catherine started, almost betraying herself in the excitement of understanding the underlying cause of his resentment. Unwittingly she had held the key to the King's unrest. This could undo him — but not yet. Clarence was not quite ready.

"My Lord," she said gently, "God knows

you have cause to be embittered but guard your tongue. England is not yet ready to accept that whispered tale of the King's bastardy. It could bring you to the block and I to the stake."

He came back to her smiling. "With you by my side I can eschew the wine cup. Can you love me, Catherine? Leave Kingsford. Of what worth is he? As my mistress you would lack for nothing. I would establish you fittingly and set no rival to mock your state." He gave a short laugh. "I am besotted and I care not. Were you free I'd wed with you."

She gave a swift intake of breath but he continued.

"Why not? My brother made no greater match. While my cousin, Warwick, arranged his betrothal to Bona of Savoy, he wed in secret at Grafton with Lord Grey's widow. England murmured but accepted her."

Catherine looked down at the rushes. "Lady Grey was a widow, sir," she reminded him gently. "I am not."

"Kingsford is but mortal."

Her eyes met his and her lips parted soundlessly.

"If I were King you would agree to be my love?"

She was evasive. "If you were King, we would both be safe, My Lord."

He drew her close and kissed her hard on the mouth. "Now God be praised. We must meet again, sweet, and soon."

"It will be difficult."

"Aye, we must be patient, and know that while we are apart, I shall be working in our interest." He considered. "There is a tavern hard by the Abbey, 'The Crossed Keys'. Do you know it?"

"I have seen it."

"Is there a man in the household you could trust to come to me?"

"My groom, Rob Wentworth."

"Send me word when you can go to the inn. The innkeeper knows me well and served in my company. Do not risk yourself. I will hold myself in readiness to come when you call but if I am late, do not delay. We will fix another meeting. Tell your man to ride hard to Coldharbour and he will not find me ungrateful."

She donned her riding gloves and he took her hand, turned it upwards and kissed her wrist. "Do not make me wait for you too long."

She smiled. "The length of time is in your hands, My Lord," then she quickly went from him into the shop to collect her mended pendant.

The King was ill and had taken to his chamber. It was an unprecedented occasion. The Palace buzzed with the news. He had taken some chill, they said, after hunting and sweated too heavily. Now his great bulk was laid low and Mistress Shore waited on him tenderly. While the attendants at Westminster rushed hither and thither on the Chamberlain's orders, Hugh's vigilance was relaxed and Catherine thought in time to risk a second illicit meeting with her royal lover. She sent Rob Wentworth, at all speed to Thames Street, arranging to go to the tavern that afternoon.

She was fortunate. It seemed that all conspired towards her wishes since Lord Hastings summoned Hugh to ride to the Tower together with several others in the King's household with messages for the sitting of the Council. She was free and with the palace in such a turmoil would not be missed if she chose to slip away unattended.

She found the Duke awaiting her all impatient. He kissed her soundly and his mood was jubilant.

"So, our Golden Edward ails? I had thought it impossible."

She sat down at his invitation, smiling at his boyish eagerness.

"You have not been in his company of late. He is overweight, unhealthily so. He rides out less frequently and imbibes too freely of the rich food and wine at the table." She flashed him one mischievous wink. "His physician warns him that His Grace's vices are like to shorten his life if he does not curtail them."

"So —" Clarence mused thoughtfully. "No wonder the Woodvilles guard Elizabeth's brood with such care. A minority would not please the merchants, though the nobles might find it opportune. With the King's brother as Lord Protector — we might fare well, my Catherine."

"You go before your horse to market. The King lives and his heirs grow."

"Aye, and the position of Protector has ever held its own dangers as Humphrey of Gloucester was to find to his cost."

She poured wine with careful deliberation. "Suppose the King's sons were not the heirs."

He had lifted the wine flagon after her. His hand jerked and wine splashed on to the table. She watched the brownish stain against the whiteness of the scrubbed boards. Once before she had thought how blood-like wine appeared when spilt. It had been at Middleham in the hall and she had sat with Gloucester.

His protruberant eyes searched her face and his loose mouth parted in eager anticipation.

"You have heard talk? Years ago it was noised secretly that the marriage to Elizabeth Woodville was no marriage. Is this your drift?"

"What did they say of it, My Lord?"

He seated himself so close that his knees touched hers and his breath fanned her cheek.

"I attempted to probe it. A singing boy was questioned. He told some garbled tale of the King's precontract with one of the Duchess's ladies —"

"One Eleanor?"

He frowned. "You have heard the tales, aye, Eleanor Butler, old Shrewsbury's daughter." He checked and gulped from the cup. "The boy was found drowned. I was unable to gauge the truth of the rumour. She disappeared into some nunnery at Norwich, I think, whether at her own wish or the King's orders, I know not."

"And she died?"

"Aye, in 1466."

"After the King's marriage with Lady Grey?"

"That is so."

"Did you believe the tale?"

He shrugged. "If it is true, the secret was well kept. At the time Stillington, Bishop of Bath and Wells, kept the privy seal."

"Was he *then* Bishop of Bath and Wells?"
He lowered the cup before drinking again. "No."

"They were indeed wed." She twisted her lip, wryly. "Edward told me himself. He said I reminded him of her, though she was dark. He was very drunk when he said it."

"By Christ's wounds, if he recalls that he told you —"

"I think he will not but it is not without the bounds of possibility."

He stared across the room, his mind racing with the enormity of her disclosure. Once, years ago, he believed he had come close to the truth of this but proof had eluded him and he had not dared face Edward with his knowledge of it.

"If there could be proof — Stillington will not speak."

"There were written contracts. Edward said that Stillington's hand shook when he handed him the quill and that his teeth chattered like dice in the cup."

"Edward would destroy the documents. He must have done for the safety of the boy's claims."

"I think, My Lord, we can be sure that one copy exists."

"Why so?"

"Why do you think Bishop Stillington still

lives and was so well rewarded?"

His eyes gleamed. "Exactly. You have hit the mark, lady. Should Stillington die and the document is discovered, the scandal would shake the realm. In his wiliness Stillington keeps the copy hidden. Even so he's a brave man. There are ways of making him talk."

"A prince of the Church, My Lord? Difficult."

"Aye." His tongue crept out snake-like and licked at his lips. "So Edward is forced to be circumspect. That must irk him sorely. As a boy he was wont to fly into passions and smash up tapestries and stools."

"Then we too must guard ourselves well."

He pulled his lower lip. "You think he is not dangerously ill?"

"He is not like to die — this time." She put her hand on his arm. "Will you wait?"

"He could live for years." He gave a brief half snort of amusement. "Why are you so hot for his blood? Does it pique you that he returns to the solicitous arms of our merry Jane?"

"No." She ran her finger round the metal rim of the wine cup. The landlord had brought out his best. No leathern jack for My Lord of Clarence. "My father was Lancastrian. He died at Tewkesbury."

He passed the matter off as if of little importance, accepting her reason without question. Since it walked well with his own desires he would not doubt her sincerity.

"But you are right, Catherine, we must take care. Watch for me at Westminster. I would know the movements of Dorset and young Richard Grey, and make yourself pleasant with Hastings. He will not think it ill since he is the King's good friend, and if the King dies I need his goodwill. He is one of the most powerful men in England."

She rose, preparatory to departure. "Speaking of powerful men, swear you will not seek to harm Gloucester."

He swung round and she saw an ugly scowl between his brows.

"Why so? He has never been a good friend to me. Edward has favoured him from childhood, granting him lands and offices above my own state. Why concern yourself about my cub of a brother?"

She went to him and reached up, placed her hands on the black velvet shoulders of his doublet. "He was kind to me. He delivered me from the living death of the nunnery at Gupshill and besides" — she kissed him lightly — "you need him. He will keep the North at rest for you."

He tightened his grip round her waist and kissed her so that her lips moved under his and bruised against her teeth.

"So he will," he said as he released her, "and I shall want leisure in Westminster for my own pleasure."

She left him then and hurried out into the shaded close, peacefully quiet against the strong grey walls of the Abbey. Deliberately she took her kerchief and wiped her mouth. She had sowed the poison. Now let it work awhile.

CHAPTER XIV

Catherine's head was bent with Cecily's over her embroidery frame when the storm broke. Hugh burst into the apartment, his face set.

"I ride to Middleham, immediately."

"On the King's business?"

He hesitated, glanced warningly at his daughter and dismissed her.

Cecily did not argue. She had learnt to obey instantly these days, knowing her father's need to talk apart with his young wife.

She loved Catherine deeply and it troubled her sorely that these two were not at peace with each other.

When she had gone, closing the door quietly, Catherine said, "What is it? Have you angered the King?"

"Not I, Clarence. He is arrested. The King has personally conveyed him to the Tower."

"On what charge?"

He shrugged. "God knows. There has been talk of risings in Cambridgeshire and Huntingdonshire. Whether Clarence is implicated is not yet known. No charges have been specified other than the usual vague accusations of speaking against the King's State, thereby endangering the peace of the realm. Since his recent illness His Grace has been beside himself. 'Tis said he consulted with seers, being over-concerned for his own recovery. The man told him some tale about his successor. His name would begin with 'G'. Since Clarence's name is George the King is further incensed."

"But surely this is some brief quarrel, soon patched up. The King and Clarence have quarrelled before. Earlier this year there was the Ankaret Cogges affair and the flare-up over Burdett and Stacey."

"This time it's serious enough. He's lodged in the Bowyer Tower. Richard must hear of it."

Catherine placed the embroidery frame on the floor by her chair. "Does the King send you?"

"No."

"Then you risk much."

He knelt down by her. "Listen, Catherine, there has been that between us of late which I would have unsaid. I hold no brief for Clarence but in this matter I think the King judges him unheard. I know Richard will wish to know the truth of it. The Woodvilles have ever wished Clarence dead. They will seek to keep Gloucester from intervening."

"You think he would?"

"They are brothers."

"But so are Clarence and the King."

"Aye."

She rose and went from him to the casement, watching the movement in the courtyard, men-at-arms, priests, monks from the Abbey.

"I think you are wise. I must stay at Westminster."

"You would wish to go with me?"

She bit her lip, turning. "I have not the Queen's leave and, as you say, the Woodvilles would be better ignorant of your purpose but— " she hesitated and then said hurriedly, "take Cecily with you. She will slow you somewhat but she rides well and you need detour only slightly to Cadeby."

"You were anxious to keep her here by you."

"I know, but now the atmosphere of the court will be fraught. It is safer if she goes. Take Margery. She loves the girl and you know Cecily dislikes Nurse."

"She will argue."

"I will persuade her."

He nodded. "You are in the right of it, but I wish you were to go with me."

"His Grace may allow me leave to go to

Coldharbour. I would comfort the children if I can."

"Gloucester will wish to ensure their safety."

"Yes." She was thinking of what she and Clarence both knew to be true. Edward's fear which threatened Clarence's children, true heirs in blood, if the Woodville marriage were proven non-lawful. Would Edward strike at young Ned and Margaret? It was unthinkable, but Edward alone was not to be feared. If the Queen's kin were aware of the facts what would they not do to safeguard the rights of young Edward of Wales and little Richard of York?

Cecily was tearful but Catherine soothed her ruffled feathers.

"Nurse will no longer have charge of you. You have Margery as your companion and it is time you oversaw for me the running of the house."

"But you will come soon?"

"Either that or we shall send for you when all is quiet again here. I promise."

Cecily hugged her tight and went reluctantly, her eyes red-rimmed. Catherine allowed Hugh to embrace her, though strive as she might, she could not return his ardour. She stifled the fear that she might not again see them and waved them "God speed" from the courtyard.

The days passed and the Court still seethed with rumours. Catherine waited in an agony of suspense. Clarence had been arrested so soon. She could not believe that he had involved himself in this rebellion in Cambridge. The rising had been quelled and its leader put to the question. He was found to be a pretender passing himself off as the Earl of Oxford, but he did not break under the torture and accuse the Duke of Clarence of having incited him to revolt. Why then was Clarence under strict guard in the Tower? Had he foolishly blurted out the truth about the Butler marriage? Stillington still walked free. If Clarence had indeed spoken, then it could not be long before the King ordered her arrest.

Lord Hastings was found to be an ally in her husband's cause. He visited her in her apartments the day following Hugh's departure.

"Pardon, Mistress Kingsford. Has Hugh ridden North to Gloucester?"

She did not seek to hide the truth from him. "He thought it best." She paused. "My husband's allegiance is to Duke Richard."

Hastings nodded, seating himself at her invitation. "I think him well advised. This is a bad business."

"My Lord, will the King release his brother?

Surely, if there is no proof of treachery —"

"Oh there has been proof in the past, more than enough but then it seemed the King had little need to fear him."

"And now he has?" She was troubled.

He frowned, lowering his voice. "The King is not himself. God knows Clarence had given him little cause to love him but in this I think the King's hand is guided by the Queen's party. There has ever been bad blood between them since the Warwick rebellion. The Queen's father and brother were executed at Coventry by Warwick when Clarence supported him. She has never forgiven him."

"You think Duke Richard will come South?"

"I pray God he does so. If any man can save Clarence it will be Richard, and if not, he can curb the King from excesses. I have tried and cannot."

She smiled at his rueful countenance. "Do not fear, My Lord. I shall respect your confidence. Will the King be angered by Hugh's departure without leave?"

"I told the King I myself sent him to York with dispatches for the levies." He rose. "To be blunt, madam, I am no more lover of the Queen's relations than Gloucester or Clarence. I would have support against their growing influence, and soon."

As he moved to the door she said hesitantly, "I am concerned for the Duke's children, sir. The King forbade my visits to Coldharbour. Would it be possible for you to request now his permission for me to see them? The little Edward is easily upset and will feel this parting from his father. It is only a short time since the pair found themselves motherless. In some respects the Lady Margaret will be more distressed since her understanding is the greater, and though a child, she is no fool."

He nodded. "I will do my best and send you word."

He was successful for the King gave permission two days later that she might go to Coldharbour. As she had imagined the state of the children was pitiful indeed. All progress she had made in chattering with the Lord Edward appeared to have been halted. He clung to her fearfully but uttered not one word. The Lady Margaret's expression was unwontedly solemn.

"Will they chop off my father's head, Catherine?" The terrible simplicity of the question brought a rush of tears to Catherine's eyes and she hugged them both to her tightly.

"Now, Lady Margaret, where did you hear such gossip? The King, your royal uncle, has your affairs well in hand. He will send for you soon and explain why you must be parted from your father for a while."

"They will not let me see him," she interrupted, her eyes wide and bright with unshed tears.

Catherine found no words to comfort her. It would be cruel to deny the possibility of the Duke's execution were he to be arraigned before Parliament and found guilty. As she was rowed back to Westminster she tried not to think of the frightened girl at Coldharbour, younger than she had been.

"I must see him." She recalled with painful clarity the awful sick fear that had paralysed her in Tewkesbury, almost making a coward of her, too afraid to see her father's last moments. For his sake, she had been prepared to torture this lovely, brilliant child. Edward, fortunately, would not understand, not yet.

She stared unseeing across the marshland of the South Bank. She had no way of knowing if her revelation of the King's secret had brought about his brother's hasty incarceration. Certainly she had openly encouraged him to take arms against the King — promised him her body and her inner strength. What state would he now be in in the Bowyer Tower? She knew her man. He would be too proud to plead and too weak to suffer to the full. He would undoubtedly take to the wine cup again for solace. Under its influence he would blurt out those things which for his own safety he should keep hidden at present.

Now she knew that she pitied Clarence, as she held grudging admiration for Edward and undying love for Richard. Please God he would come soon. Richard would beg the King to do what was best for the children.

By the end of October he was in London, lodging with his mother at the old Yorkist stronghold of Baynard's Castle. Catherine waited anxiously for sight of him and for news of her husband, but though Gloucester at once sought and was granted immediate audience with his brother, he delayed making any appearance at the Court festivities and she was denied sight of him.

Once or twice she found the Queen's eyes fixed on her speculatively. On one occasion so distressed was she that she stabbed her finger viciously with her embroidery needle, marring the chaste white silk of the altar cloth with great gouts of blood. She felt utterly alone now and vulnerable. Hugh had not returned from Middleham. He sent her greetings by Gloucester's guard captain. The Duke had sent him North to Berwick but he hoped to come to Westminster for Christmas. Cecily was established safely at Kingsford and Janet now almost restored to health.

The ladies who were her companions in the

Queen's service did not invite her confidences. She knew the cause. She had held the King's favour and it made her at once an object of respect but also of envy. They treated her with due courtesy, but she could trust not one of them. Finding Margery had gone to Kingsford with her stepdaughter, the Queen provided Catherine with a new maid, Molly Tiverton, somewhat untidy in appearance but efficient and respectful. Catherine could not rid herself of the vague fear that the girl was there to spy on her.

Determined to discover anything she could pertaining to Clarence's arrest, Catherine, one afternoon, free from her duties in attendance, went to "The Crossed Keys" with Rob Wentworth. The landlord was distressed by what had happened to his former master but was clearly unwilling to talk of anything other than normal civilities.

As they re-entered the palace courtyard, Rob bent respectfully to whisper to her.

"Mistress, did you note yon fellow in the green jerkin? He was lounging outside 'The Crossed Keys'. I noted him as we left. I believe he is in the service of the Marquess of Dorset."

They exchanged anxious glances. She thanked him and dismissed him.

Dorset — concerned with her coming and

goings? Did he suspect that she knew? Fear pricked at her spine again. What had Clarence said, the singing boy he had been anxious to question had been found drowned in the river. How easily that could be her fate, perhaps more merciful than arrest. If she were to be put to the question — ? Her face whitened. It could not be. The King would not dare accuse her. And yet — she was of no importance. Unlike the Duke of Clarence, her disappearance would cause only momentary enquiry. Assuredly she was in danger.

She dressed with care for dinner in the hall, parrying skilfully Molly Tiverton's chattered questions as to her destination during the afternoon. She stared at her reflection in the glass before presenting herself at the Queen's apartments. She looked wan and pale. She would need to put on a bolder face tonight.

As she entered the hall behind the Queen, she faltered and almost stumbled. Gloucester was seated beside the King and he rose to bow courteously and greet his royal sister-in-law with a hearty kiss. His grey eyes met Catherine's fleetingly, acknowledging her with a faint bow. She seated herself in her place well down the table, striving to hide her agitation. It was hard to see him from here, but in those few moments, she had registered all she wished to know.

He looked pale, a little tired and strained, but well enough. So he was not finding it easy to convince the King. Edward took great pains to honour him. It was the first time Catherine had seen them together. God, how she longed to kiss away those frown lines, deepening now between his brows. What he must suffer, loving Edward dearly and yet at odds with him in his treatment of Clarence.

She had not expected him to single her out but late in the evening he came to her side, courteous as ever.

"I trust you are well, Mistress Kingsford. I regret I was forced to keep Hugh from your side."

She curtsied low, her legs trembling in the bewildering chaos of her love. He was here and near her. God had surely answered her prayers. If she were to die, and she could not doubt it, she had seen him again and he had not forgotten her.

"I thank Your Grace, I am well. Hugh writes his need to stay in Berwick."

He frowned. "The air of London does not agree with you, I fear. You look pale, mistress."

She smiled gamely. "I think I tire of the late feasting," then quietly, "how are Her Grace the Duchess and little Edward?"

"Both well." His expression had lightened at her talk of Middleham but grew grave again as her words had prompted some new concern.

"I hear you saw His Grace of Clarence's children recently. How are they?"

He put his hand gently on her arm and led her some way apart.

"Your Grace, I entreat you to beg the King to take them into his care — or yours. They should not be left to the care of attendants at Coldharbour. The Lady Margaret fears for her father, natural enough, but she is older than her years and knows the gravity of the situation. As for little Edward —" She broke off with a half sob.

He nodded. "Aye, I thought as much. I have requested that Ned allow me to take the children back to Middleham until George —" He shrugged wearily. "At least until the charges are specified and the trial opened."

"You think it will come to that?"

He regarded her directly, noting her increased pallor.

"You have some interest in my brother's affairs?"

"Who would not, my lord, a royal prince —"

She sought to avoid those cool grey eyes of his. She felt they had bored through to her own guilt, but he said nothing.

"Unfortunately His Grace the King has given the children into the care of the Marquess of Dorset."

Catherine rocked on her feet. Dorset? The Queen's son by her first husband. If Clarence should perish, could the children be either safe or happy in Dorset's custody?

"You were about to say something, mistress?" Gloucester's voice was cool.

She shook her head. She dare tell him nothing of her suspicions and she knew well enough he had tried every method of persuasion he knew to alter the King's decision but without success.

The autumn passed into winter. The holy season came and went. Hugh did not arrive for the festivities nor did Gloucester seek to return to Yorkshire. He came rarely to Court, and Catherine was forced to be content only with glimpses of his slight frame, elegantly clad but without extravagance. He did not again seek her out for private talk and she knew his dislike of the Queen made him chary of presenting himself in her company.

Rob Wentworth warned Catherine of their spy's continued interest.

"When we leave the palace he always follows, mistress," he said worriedly. "You must take care with whom you talk and never go anywhere without me in attendance."

Catherine passed off his anxiety as lightly as she dared. "The King fears for my safety now that my husband cannot protect me. It is likely he has set a guard."

"More likely a jailer, madam." He shook his head as her lip trembled. "I'd not trust yon man with a woman nor his fellow ruffians."

"You have seen others?"

"Aye."

"But, Rob, what can they want?"

He regarded her steadily. "You'd know that better than I, mistress."

She drew in her lips. "Rob, if you would leave my service —"

"Not I, mistress. The master set me to serve you. I'll do that, but let me do the job properly. Go nowhere without me."

Parliament assembled on January 16 and a cold, wet day it was. Now at last the truth was out and the Duke of Clarence formally accused before the bar of the house. Since London was agog with the scandal and all tongues whispered that it was the Queen's influence that had brought the King to accuse his brother, Elizabeth kept to her apartments.

Catherine sat near her chair, reading, playing the lute, anything which would calm the Queen. She was not wont to be so nervous.

Towards evening she sent Catherine to question if the King was yet in his apartments. My Lord of Hastings nodded his answer.

"His Grace is wearied. He will eat in his own chamber tonight."

"How did it go, My Lord?"

"Badly. The King himself addressed Parliament. He accused the Duke of desiring to dethrone him, with dealing with wizards and sorcerers. He brought forth the old charge of unlawfully seizing the persons of Ankaret Twynhoe and Thursby and both trying and condemning them without the authority of the King's justice." He passed a weary hand over his brow. "He brought forward evidence to show that the Duke had supplied his servants with money to provide wine and venison with the express purpose of feasting the common people royally, that they would regard him with favour."

"But, My Lord, many might be accused of such crimes."

"The King does not forget his brother's past treachery. Clarence has spoken unwisely. He has thrown disrespect on the King, charging him with being no son of the Duke of York, even in so doing bringing his own mother's reputation into disrepute." He sighed. "It was even said that Clarence was involved in these latest rebellions and has sworn to redress the wrongs to those defeated Lancastrian lords, and if he should gain the throne, restore to them their former lands and honours."

"What did the Duke say in his own defence? Was he allowed to speak?"

Hastings grinned ruefully. "It was impossible to prevent him. He stormed at Edward, there before them all, reiterated his innocence and challenged Edward to single combat to try before God whose words were truthful."

"In God's name what prompted him to such stupidity?"

"What indeed?" Hastings was grim. "No one spoke for him. The shameful scene horrified the whole gathering. Council has not yet forgotten Clarence's bursting in on their deliberations to protest against Burdett's and Stacey's executions. That too was taken into account."

"Will they find him guilty?"

Hastings shook his head. "The trial will drag on days yet, but I fear there is but one end to this affair."

The Queen listened intently when Catherine delivered her news and took calmly enough the King's refusal to come to her, though as it appeared a blunt statement of his belief that she was involved in his attack on his brother and rather intimated that he regretted his need to proceed, it would have been more circumspect to have supported his wife on this night.

Catherine lay wide awake. Molly Tiverton now slept on a truckle-bed in her room, so she had to watch herself even at night. So far there was no indication that Clarence had attacked the King's marriage. Would he do so in open court? It was likely. If it was as Hastings had said, this heated brawling between them, would either know, in his rage, what he said to the other?

The trial dragged on and little was spoken concerning it by those about the Queen except in whispers. Catherine made no attempt to leave the palace. Gloucester did not feast with the Court at Westminster though it was rumoured that he attended all the sessions of the trial, sitting white-faced and grimly silent. He had several times been closeted privately with the King and Catherine did not doubt that he had pleaded for his brother's life.

One piece of conversation she overheard which further increased her misery. Sir Richard Grey, the Queen's younger stepson, was muttering in a corner of the solar with a knight called Vaughan, a man she had not known well, but understood to be of the Queen's party and in the direct service of Earl Rivers. She had returned unexpectedly to look for a book the Queen had left behind, before retiring to her chamber. The room was in semi-darkness, the candles having not yet been lighted. The two men were seated near the fire and were so engrossed in their talk they did not at first notice her.

"It will be all over by the morning and Clarence condemned. That wily ambassador, Le Roux, finally convinced Edward the man must die."

The older man, Vaughan, chuckled. "Aye, it was a master stroke. The Spider insisted he had it on good authority that Clarence's desire to wed Mary of Burgundy was merely one more step towards the English throne. Certainly it would have given him the means to make the attempt."

Grey moved his beringed hands nearer to the blaze. "I had not thought Edward would believe him so readily. God's teeth, even I would not think Clarence could be really such a fool as to again give his allegiance to Margaret of Anjou."

"What could it gain him?"

"Little enough, but the suggestion is sharp enough to further enrage Edward. This time Clarence will die."

He turned sharply as Catherine struck an unwary foot against a foot-stool in the gloom of the darkening chamber. "What is it?"

She curtsied. "Your pardon, Sir Richard, the Queen sent me for a book."

He frowned as she peered round uncertainly. "Oh, there it is, thank you." Vaughan handed her the slender, leather-bound volume. "My apologies, sir," and she was gone.

In the corridor she stood with her back against the door, her breast heaving, striving to keep back her tears. What had she done? There seemed no way now in which that vain foolish man could extricate himself from the web they'd spun for him. Now, too late, she understood the full horror of Margaret's cry: "Will they cut off my father's head?"

She had seen her own father die and she had thought naught could satisfy her but the spilt blood of those responsible, but it was not so. It could achieve nothing but fear and anguished pain to those children, younger, more vulnerable than she had been at Tewkesbury.

"What is it, Mistress Kingsford? Are you not well?"

She started. It was unbelievable that Gloucester had come upon her suddenly, and she not aware of it.

She struggled to recover mastery of herself. "Your pardon, sir. I am somewhat distressed, as we all are, to hear the ill news of the trial."

"Are you not anxious to see the King's enemies brought to justice?"

His tone was brusque and she stared at his

serious face, lit by a lighted brand some way off down the corridor, throwing into stark relief, his eyes darkened with anxiety and the mouth held in, in that grimace of pain she knew well.

"Is My Lord of Clarence indeed the King's enemy?" she whispered.

"It seems so since he is found guilty and condemned to a traitor's death."

"God help him." She put her hand to her breast to still the sudden agonized leap of her heart.

"The King will not allow it."

He shrugged. "He said no word but left the court immediately. However, there is time yet."

"My Lord, will you plead for him?"

He bent towards her, the glare of his eyes almost frightening pools of blackness, unwontedly dark. She could not believe them his own grey ones she knew so well.

"Who was there to plead eloquently for your father, Catherine? Would you really have me do this, or is your concern merely feigned?"

"God have mercy on my soul if I lie, sir. I beg you to do what you can."

He stepped back and at once seemed normal again, tired, disturbed, but no longer the challenging judge under whose gaze many prisoners must quail.

"God knows I have tried," he said quietly, "and I shall try again."

"When — ?" she queried through stiffened lips. "Who will speak to the children?"

"It is not determined. The King has delayed in signing the death warrant." He put out his hand to lead her along the corridor. "Give your heart peace, Catherine, the children will be safe enough. Ned will not seek to strike out at them and I shall be there to see they are not deprived of their rights, but Clarence is attainted. Both he and his heirs have lost any claims on the throne. Perhaps, in a sense, it is just and right that it should be so."

As she reached the door of the Queen's apartments and he moved off to seek audience with the King, she lingered, biting her lip. God, if he only knew. If the King's children were bastards, and Clarence and his heirs under attainder, then he, Richard, was the heir to England. He could not know — he must not know. If once he was aware of it, his life would be as much in peril as Clarence's for Catherine knew Edward. Even loving Richard as he did he would not hesitate for one second to strike down the man who could take from his own children the right to sit in St. Edward's chair. He had fought too long and too hard for that.

CHAPTER XV

Catherine blew on her hands impatiently as she stared round the entrance to Caxton's shop. The apprentice had assured her he would be quick about his errand, and at any other time she would have been fascinated by the leather-bound copies of books, gold tooled, which had been lain open on the counter for the perusal of customers. Above she could hear the click of the compositors at work assembling the lines of type and the muttered talk of the craftsmen and apprentices. The Queen had been promised a copy of the "Dictes and Sayings of the Philosophers" which had been translated from the French by Lord Rivers. It had been a Christmas gift but there had been some error on one of the pages and the Queen had dispatched Catherine with Molly in attendance to bring the corrected book to her apartments.

She was out of sorts and waspish these days since the King rarely came to her side and the gossip of the Court was of nothing but the projected execution of the Duke of Clarence, sentence of death having been passed by a special court under the youthful Duke of Buckingham who had been appointed High Steward simply for this purpose. She was angered by the antagonism of the Duchess of York who had come to Westminster and pleaded on her knees for remittance of the terrible sentence of disemboweling. Edward had given way. The Duke was to be beheaded privately, within the walls of the Tower, but yet he held his hand and Commons had petitioned him to execute the due sentence of the court.

Catherine was dispirited and cold. She would have given anything to be away from prying eyes, safe in her own chamber, but she had no privacy these days. The Queen had been in such haste that she had had no time to summon Rob Wentworth to accompany them, but the way was very short, there were still people about in plenty and she had Molly Tiverton with her.

The apprentice returned with the book carefully wrapped in silk, bowed and respectfully held open the door for the Queen's lady and her maid. Outside the ground was hard, the sky pewter grey. Catherine drew her cloak tightly round her.

"Come, Molly, the sooner we are before the fire in the parlour the better."

"Yes, indeed, madam." The maid looked

back towards the shop. "Poor lad. Did you note his hands were red-raw with the cold? It cannot be easy to handle the type in these conditions. I think I do not remember so bitter a February. Some say the river will freeze if it continues."

They both wore pattens over their shoes and they were cumbersome, impeding the way. Catherine lifted her skirts to watch her steps on the slippery ground. They were near to "The Crossed Keys". She was half inclined to seek a cup of mulled ale but it would be wiser to hasten. The Queen would grumble if she delayed and in all events she was not escorted. She hurried ahead expecting that the more weighty Molly would grumble somewhat at her increased speed. She could hear the sound of the maid's shambling steps behind her, then a sudden animal cry and a slithering noise of a falling body.

She turned immediately to find Molly crouched upon the ground clasping at her left ankle.

"Mistress, I'm sorry. I slipped on the ice."

Catherine looked hastily round for assistance. "Molly, how bad is it? Does it pain you?" She knelt to examine the injury for herself.

The girl winced sharply as her fingers probed the stockinged foot. "Please, oh please, madam, don't —"

"You can't stay here, girl. You'll freeze to death. Try to stand and throw your weight on me."

"Madam, I can't." The girl wailed shrilly as Catherine stooped to take her hand and made the attempt to get her to stand.

"Now, Molly, you can. Don't put weight on the bad foot, though I do not think it is broken. Remember I know something of injuries since my days in the convent. If you can hop back to the inn, we can get help." She peered round hopefully a second time, but since she had entered the shop the lane had cleared. No one was in sight. Although it was still early, all passers-by had sought shelter from the piercing stabs of the icy wind. "I do not like to leave you alone even for a moment, but if you really cannot stand I'll go either to the shop or the inn and bring someone to lift you." She turned. "I think 'The Crossed Keys' is nearer, but I should feel easier in my mind if you would try to get there with me."

Molly made a feeble attempt to stand, clinging to Catherine's fingers, but she gasped with the painful effort and subsided again on the hard-packed ground.

"I cannot."

"Then you must stay. Take the book, I will

only be moments."

She gave a final worried glance at the huddled maid and went as quickly as the slippery ground would allow towards the inn where she had once met Clarence. Fortunately the innkeeper knew her well and would not hesitate to come to her assistance.

Even before she reached the building she was thankful to see two figures moving towards her.

She floundered toward them thankfully.

"Oh, sirs, can you help me? My maid has fallen. She cannot stand. Will one of you help to convey her to the inn? I will pay you well."

They came towards her, the taller hastening ahead of his companion.

Thankful that she had no need to proceed further she turned and began to lead them towards her injured maid.

"It is not far. She is not too heavy —"

The man grunted as he came behind her and at that moment she too slipped. He caught her as she sought to recover herself and she murmured her thanks, then tried to withdraw in order to lead him round the angle of the Abbey wall back to Molly.

Surprisingly his arms tightened round her and she struggled angrily. So the man intended to use this excuse to subject her to mishandling.

"Let me go, sir. I said I would pay you with money, not to allow liberties with my person."

She expected him to laugh and make some bawdy jest but he did neither. Before she could make a further move or cry out his hand clapped down hard over her mouth. She was lifted from the ground and felt herself borne along at greater speed. She struggled and fought, kicked at his shins, but it was useless. He was ready for the pain of her blows and held her grimly. He said nothing to the man behind and even in her panic she knew that the abduction was planned. The men had been ready for her. It was even possible that the Queen had sent her out on this errand for that very purpose. The men had hidden themselves and waited for her. Though cold terror struck at her she did not abate her struggles.

Then she heard the running steps of the man following, a clash of iron against iron and a shout.

"Bite his hand, mistress. Make him drop you, anything. I'll tackle this one. Then run."

Rob — and near enough to call for help. She gave a sob of thankfulness but what could he do? There were two and obviously trained men. His instructions had been clear enough.

She bit down with vicious savagery on to the hard hand which silenced her. The man gave a dull roar of pain and fury. It had worked. For one second he released his grip to try to ease his injured hand. She had the presence of mind to seize her opportunity and turned quickly and kicked him where she knew it would be most effective. His first bellow was naught to the scream of agony which followed. He doubled up and she waited for no more but tore off into the shadows which were creeping now across the wall of the Abbey. She ran blindly, panting and slipping on the hard ground. She dare not return to the palace and her attackers barred the way to the inn. There would be sanctuary in the Abbey Church. What man would dare to attack a helpless woman within? Surely there would be a priest in attendance at this hour but Rob — could she leave him to the mercy of her assailants? Her only hope for him was to get assistance.

She dashed on following the Abbey wall to the North gate, tore at it and stumbled along the broad sanctuary, collapsing at last in the porchway of the Great West door. She had no wind to take her further and she crouched there on the stone seat, sobbing. How long she stayed there she did not know. She could not summon the strength to open the heavy door. Then she felt a touch on her arm and opened her mouth to scream.

"Mistress, it's me, Rob."

"Rob." She clung to the rough frieze of his sleeve, sobbing her relief against the leather of his jerkin. "Thank God. I thought they would kill you."

"Aye, well the first was no match for me and the second you'd incapacitated." He gave the strangled ghost of a laugh. "Where did they teach you such skills? I doubt in the convent, lady."

"They'll follow."

He shook his head. "The first'll not follow ever again and the second not for some time. I laid him out with the pommel of my dagger. He was still retching and groaning." He stooped as she felt wetness on his sleeve. "It's naught to concern you — a flesh wound only. He blooded me early. Lady, can you walk?"

"Yes, but shouldn't we go into the Abbey? You are hurt and spent."

"No. There's no safety there."

"But —"

"They were King's men, lady. Even if we were granted temporary sanctuary it could not be for long. I must get you away."

Her eyes dilated in the darkness of the porch. "Molly?"

He sheathed his dagger and as she handed him a torn portion of her cloak, tied it firmly round the wound in his upper arm which oozed blood sluggishly.

"Molly will take care of herself. I think she deliberately feigned the injury."

"But —"

"Come, mistress, we must go. We'd best head for the river. I'll not risk the King's Stairs, we must edge our way through the West door and make for the mill wharf. Can you walk?"

"Yes." She nodded and rose at once, fully aware of the need not to hinder him.

They redoubled their tracks back towards Canton's Red Pale and followed the shell of the Abbey wall. Fortune favoured them, as it had served her an ill chance earlier. There were still few people about. It seemed a long way by the mill ditch, floundering and struggling along, hampered by her patterns and the fullness of her court gown until he halted and drew her close behind him.

"This is where the men-at-arms drill but it's deserted at the moment. Stay well back against the wall while I look for a ferryman."

She tried to call him back and give him gold but he was gone, melting into the greyness of the river mist. Now the first shock was over, she found herself trembling, so that she had to cling to the rough stones of the wall to keep her feet. Her teeth were chattering and even now she could not think beyond the immediate necessity to obey Rob and find a boat. She did not try to think, only to endure.

He came back at last, reaching for her hand to lead her. "Come. I've had to steal one."

"Rob?" She drew back. "You'll hang for this. Leave me."

"I can't, mistress. I've killed one of the King's men. It's useless to think of return now. We must get down river. Can you row?"

She shook her head.

"Never mind, I'll manage but I'm hampered by this damned scratch on my arm."

The river seemed black and oily, menacing. She shivered despite herself when he drew her into the flimsy cockle-shell of the boat, but sat still in the stern, as he instructed as he cast off and began to row steadily into midstream. After a while he left off rowing and allowed the current to carry them and eased his aching muscles.

"Are you cold?"

"Yes, no — it doesn't matter. Oh Rob, what are we going to do?"

"I daren't risk the river race at London Bridge. I'd best take you to the South Bank. Have you money?"

"A little," she faltered. "But —"

He went on grimly. "There's a place I know. It's not what you're used to and I'd not take you there except at great need, but it will do for the present."

"Rob," she strove to keep her voice firm. "Rob, I know why those men attacked me, or at least I think I do. There is terrible danger for you, if you stay with me."

"Aye, I know." He took up the oars again. "That man I killed is in Dorset's pay. They've been watching you for days. You were mad to go to 'The Crossed Keys' that day to meet His Grace of Clarence."

She let out a long breath. "How — how did you know where I was? I — I was told to hurry and could not send for you."

"I saw you cross the court with Molly. I followed. At first I thought you'd gone to 'The Crossed Keys'. I soon discovered you hadn't."

His voice bore an odd note and she said hastily, "Rob? — I don't understand."

"I know you don't. I burst in on their handiwork. The landlord and his wife both dead on the sanded floor of the taproom. It wasn't a pretty sight."

She covered her face in her hands. "Oh no. God — I have much to answer for."

"Nay, mistress, those fellows kill without reason and that innkeeper was no better than the usual cut-throat. Don't weep for him. Save your tears for yourself. I was near the big ale cask. I'd opened the door quietly as it happens, and those two came down the stairs. It seemed they'd ransacked the place. They left and I followed. I think they'd taken rather too long over their first job for they were in haste to catch up with you. It may well be that that was why I was able to take the first by surprise. In the ordinary way I think they'd have done for me between them."

The house he had mentioned was as unprepossessing as its owner, so much so that Catherine drew back apace and had to be coaxed by Rob to cross the threshold. She knew she was now in the fetid stews of Bankside, a district filled largely with brothels and low taverns. The woman who greeted Rob with more surprise than pleasure was an elderly harridan, enormously fat and clad only in a torn, stained and shapeless shift. Her features were swollen and her small eyes lost in the huge rolls of fat. Her eyes peered at Catherine suspiciously and she ran a dirty hand through her scanty hair, brassily yellow, likely enough bleached with cow's urine.

"You're early." She sniffed. "Come to think of it we've seen little of you lately. Did you think to bring your own harlot? I tell you, lad, she's out of your class and unlike to give you good bed-sport."

"Shut it," he said harshly and she lifted her huge shoulders in an enigmatic shrug and let them fall, her pendulous breasts shaking, jelly-like, under the thin folds of her shift. "We need a place to hide. I'll pay you."

She had closed the rickety door with a bang and pointed towards the steps which led upwards to what could be little more than a barn-like attic.

"Who from?"

As they moved to climb, Rob's hand steadying her arm, the woman's casual question arrested him.

"Does it matter?"

She shrugged again. "It might, if it's dangerous."

"It's dangerous."

Catherine shuddered as he did not seek to hide their plight from this unsavoury creature.

"Are they seeking you — or her?"

"Both of us."

She made no answer and waddled towards a door which presumably led into a kitchen, for indescribable stinks came from its direction.

"Stay up there. I'll bring you food — if you pay."

Rob said gently, "Up you go, mistress. Watch yourself at the top. It will be dark up there and the shutters across."

She scrambled into the low raftered room

and she felt him spring lightly after her and move to the casement. It was fast locked and had not been opened for months for it withstood his efforts but at last purer air came in and he threw back the wooden shutters.

It was not as bad as she had thought. There was a truckle bed which she avoided with a shudder staring horrified at the stained and filthy blanket flung over it, two wooden stools and the rushes on the floor were tolerably clean. It seemed that the attic was rarely used. She sank on to one of the stools and pulled at the strings of her cloak. Thank God she wore a simple coif and hood and no high hennin which would have proclaimed her of the court.

Rob unceremoniously yanked up the soiled straw mattress and blanket and hurled them through the casement, swept up a pile of fresher straw from the floor and drew her cloak over the whole.

"Rest here, mistress. I'll see if I can find some food fit for you to try and a tolerably clean blanket. You'll be cold here and she'll not have a brazier."

She was shivering more from shock than the cold.

"I shall be well enough, Rob. Don't worry. I'm not hungry."

"You will be, later."

"Can you trust her?"

He shook his head. "No, but she's likely enough to lie for us if we pay, as much as she is to those who enquire about us."

"Will they seek us — here?"

He frowned. "Mistress, if they are so anxious to silence you, they'll seek everywhere but it will take time and that's in our favour."

"They will miss you."

"Aye."

"Have you brought any of your companions here?"

"No."

"Rob," she said pitifully, "what shall we do?"

"We must get clear of Westminster and the city. Have you ready gold?"

"I told you, only a little. I haven't the King's pearl with me — only two rings but —"

"We could not sell those. They'd track us by them." He held out a hand. "Let me see what you have."

She had four rose nobles and five silver groats. He handed back the silver and one noble.

"When that haridan demands payment do not show the gold. She'd have your throat cut for it. Pay her in silver. I'll wait awhile and then try to hire or buy two horses. You ride well and our only hope is to get free before we are hunted to this bolthole."

"What then?"

He shrugged. "I don't know. You'll not dare to go near your husband. There is work and enough for me to be had, though it's a hard time of year."

"I cannot live off you, Rob."

"You can cook and clean?"

She nodded.

"Good skills find employment. Worry first about our escape and the rest later." He rose. "I'm going below to have the arm tended."

"Let me do it."

"No — there's another below who'll see to my needs. Stay close." He grinned shamefacedly. "If you hear laughter and noise below, give no heed."

"I know where I am."

He smiled. "Mistress, you've a good heart. If I have to have feminine company in this plight I'd not have another but yours."

"Rob," she looked up at him steadily. "I cannot reward you except with my thanks."

"That is enough, mistress."

"Not nearly enough. I think you do not yet know your peril."

"I've a fair notion of it. I want to know no State secrets. If I'm taken I've less to divulge. I tell you I'd keep naught back if put to the question. As it is, we've naught to fear as I don't know what makes My Lord Marquess wish to put you safely below ground."

She lay back on the bed exhausted as he lumbered his way below and she heard him call peremptorily to the woman in the kitchen.

CHAPTER XVI

Catherine stifled a scream as something touched her. Was it a rat? She had seen them earlier in the day though, thankful to say, they appeared unlikely to attack and as much afraid of her as she was of them.

"Gently, mistress. It's I, Rob."

She sat up, pushing back her hair and attempting to smooth her clothes as she pushed the blanket aside.

"I'm sorry, Rob. I'm terrified of the least thing. Last night —" she broke off, her lip trembling pitifully.

"I know, mistress. I would have spared you that if I could. I've brought food. You must eat."

The house had wakened to full life after dark. She had lain crouched against the wall as the obscene shouts and laughter came up from below. The street door was constantly opened and Catherine could not but believe that each time it might admit the King's men. Worse than that there had come rowdy bangings on her door, commands to open up, owlish, drunken voices asking to know the name of the whore who kept herself so carefully apart from them. At last Rob had returned and all night he'd stayed on a stool near the door wary in case some more determined intruder attempted to batter his way in.

Not until morning had she fallen into an exhausted stupor.

He ate greedily and she smiled at his returned confidence. His wound had stiffened the arm, but was healing. She'd examined it.

"I must leave you to look for horses. I dare not leave it too late."

She tightened her lips, putting a brave smile on her terror.

"Of course you must go, but be careful for your own safety. If the street is searched, don't come back. Keep well away, Rob."

He nodded. "It's not likely yet awhile, but we would be missed early — and the boat —"

"Could we be traced by that?"

"I hid it close by some steps further upstream. While I'm out keep the door barred. Admit no one. You know my voice. Open to me alone." As he moved to the stair he said, "Don't show yourself at the casement."

She tortured herself with the fear of his arrest. There would be a hue and cry for them, but they would look for a man and woman. While alone he was safer. She asked herself desperately if she had the right to encumber

him with her person. When he came back with the horses she would divide her wealth with him and beg him to ride off alone. True he had killed a man-at-arms and injured a second but what would the King care for that? She was his prey and even out of the city she could not comfort herself with the belief that she would be safe. Her description was too clear. Rob knew, in his heart, it would be hard to hide a gentlewoman in a kitchen or dairy. Hadn't Anne of Gloucester found this clearly enough?

Would they murder her secretly? It seemed the best course. Like the singing boy who'd witnessed Edward's marriage to Dame Eleanor Butler her body would be found in the river or in some alley. At the moment she was almost too tired and dispirited to care — but supposing they dragged her back to some dungeon and questioned her with iron or rope — ? She was almost violently sick at the thought, yet it could not be discounted.

She was known to have associated with Clarence and would be thought to know names of accomplices in any planned rising, or information concerning arms and supplies. Edward would not dare to charge her openly with her treason but he was vindictive. She had lain beside him, he had opened his heart to her and she had betrayed him with another man and that man his despised brother. That would stick in his craw. She could not believe she would die easy.

At least Clarence would die cleanly. She wondered how he faced these dreaded, lonely hours in the Tower waiting for the end. At least her father had not had to wait. A quick shrive and a long drop was what all condemned men craved. She prayed now that it would come so to the man who'd brought her father to his death by his criminal carelessness. "Let him not be craven," she prayed, "do not let him shame his blood."

Gloucester would know by now of her complicity with his brother. Had he guessed at her determination to bring Clarence down? He had questioned her sharply enough and she knew, that if he saw need, he would hunt her down as relentlessly as the King's men.

Tears dripped on to her clasped hands, and she wiped them impatiently away. She was craven herself, kneeling here allowing depression to engulf her while Rob worked for her deliverance. Even Edward had admired her spirit as Richard had suspected her too easy submission. They were right. She was not yet dead and should she live through this, she still had the fatal key which could destroy Edward's heirs. Was he not most culpable? If Clarence had betrayed her father, it had been by accident, not by intent, but the King had been determined to make an example of the Lancastrian Lords. She could not now blame Hugh for aught and was thankful he was well away from this broil and could not be involved in her guilt.

It seemed that Rob had been gone some time, but the hours lengthened into days when one was alone and afraid. She settled herself on the bed again and resolved to think out a plan of action. Should she seek sanctuary in some convent? It was one way but she knew now that her blood flamed too hot and her flesh was too weak to find peace within convent walls — sooner a hard life, working with her hands and subject to the hard discipline of some bad-tempered mistress than that.

She sat up abruptly as she heard the sound of hooves below in the street. During the day, the whole district seemed to close in on itself, few went out of the ill-built, rat-infested hovels and few customers, even at night, rode to their pleasures. Had Rob returned with their mounts? She checked herself resolutely from going to the window. He had warned her against that, but surely there seemed too many below and she heard the clink of spurs and ring of iron swords. There were men in the street systematically searching the houses.

Catherine withdrew to the corner of the room furthest away from the casement, her body pressed hard against the wall. It was impossible for her to find any means of escape. Last night before the customers arrived Rob had forced the rickety door across the entrance to the attic. It had been removed by some impatient client and the attic had been open to the stairs but the improvised door provided privacy rather than security. It would keep out no one and lie as she might, if a search was in progress the old woman would be forced to open up. Catherine gathered up the remnants of her courage to step out willingly rather than be dragged like a rat from a hole. There was one mercy, Rob had not returned. Please God he remained clear for hours yet. He had gold and the horses. They would stand him in good stead.

The street had woken to angry life. Harlots needed good sleep during the day. What right had fool soldiers to force them from the rest to answer stupid questions? And they *were* pointless. What lord's wife would seek refuge in such a hole?

When the blow sounded on the outer door Catherine heard her landlady lumber towards it, her voice querulous.

"All right, all right. Why can't a body sleep as usual? By all the Saints what a pother after some poor thief."

"Open up." The command was peremptory. Catherine noted it was not followed by the customary "In the King's name". Her arrest would not be by due process of the law. Instructions had been given to keep the matter quiet. The inhabitants of these mean streets did not gossip. They had secrets of their own to keep.

"What do you want?" Catherine imagined the woman's defiant attitude from the tone of her voice.

"Out of the way. I want to search."

"On whose authority?" The woman's voice was shrilly self-righteous.

"On my own. Like to challenge it?"

The woman gave way, muttering sullenly and Catherine heard the man throw open the door to the kitchen. From where she was crouched she could hear the rise and fall of voices but not what was said. Obviously he was questioning the kitchen drab who tended the pots. Then she heard his voice become louder as he emerged again into the corridor at the foot of the stairs.

"Turn out your girls, old woman. I want to inspect them. Come on — all of them."

"Oh yes?" Her voice had gained its former insolence. "You've come at the wrong time for that. My clients pay good money for what you want."

He sounded grimly amused. "I'd choose a cleaner establishment than this for my entertainment. I want to look at them, not sample their talents."

Now Catherine heard the plaintive complaints of those roused from their late sleep. Bodies scrambled from truckle beds and cots and one called to another to enquire what was wrong. Was there fire, threat of plague?

Catherine knew she should go down and give herself up. While she delayed there was danger to Rob. At any moment he would return and be taken with her. She could hear the officer in charge moving from one cubicle to another and the saucy answers of the girls.

She unbarred the door and paused near the head of the stairs.

"What is it? When I came I thought this a respectable tavern."

There was a hastily checked burst of strident laughter at her words.

The man-at-arms looked up at her from the gloom of the corridor.

"Are you Catherine Kingsford?"

"And if I am?" She forced herself to descend with what dignity she could still command.

"I have orders to take you into protective

custody." The words were ironic. She noted as she reached him that he wore no badge of livery. Just so. It was not to be expected, but he was armed with sword and dagger and attired for brawling, if need be, in leathern jack and salet.

"Then I had best go with you. I cannot think why my liberty should be curtailed but I think that will be explained to me later."

He attempted no force but nodded respectfully enough.

She was anxious to leave now before Rob might return.

"Here, my good woman, lodging fee."

She pressed the single noble into the woman's hand and her eyes implored her silence concerning her companion. The woman's hand closed over it greedily before the officer could assess its worth.

"There's plenty for the purpose, mistress," she said, "more than enough."

"Then see your friends fêted tonight."

The blubber mouth contorted in what might have been a smile and could have been an expression of sympathy.

"I'll see our friends benefit, right enough."

She would warn Rob and that was all that was needful.

The man's eyes passed over her disheveled state and she flushed. "I have nothing to bring.

I'm ready to leave."

As he threw the door wide she saw two more men outside watching. He took no chances. "Will you ride pillion, mistress?"

She nodded, stiff-lipped. So they would take her to the Tower or some other prison. She had hoped it might be quick and secret, before she was aware of its coming.

He cupped his hands for her to mount and she was about to step up when she heard running steps and panted gasps. A man and in haste. Oh God, not Rob. She turned in the moment that he rounded the corner of the alley. Their eyes met and she entreated him silently to pass on, pretend his haste did not concern her, but she saw he would not. He came on, his eyes enquiring.

One of the guards checked his advance. "Hey, you, do you live in this street?"

"I lodge here. What's wrong, friend?"

The guard spoke softly to his officer. "He said there was one with her, a groom."

The captain indicated that Catherine was to mount. "Take him."

Rob struggled in the soldier's grip and Catherine came to his aid. "Why do you arrest him? What has he done?"

"If he has done naught, he'll be released, never fear, as you will be, lady."

Rob struggled, putting a brave face on it.

He was walking so he had apparently failed in his errand.

"Very well, captain. I'll ride pillion with your man. I'll not leave the lady, in all events."

Foolish, gallant Rob, to condemn himself in a few simple words. Her eyes were blinded with a rush of tears as the captain gave the command to mount and urged his horse towards the river.

CHAPTER XVII

It seemed only a short ride to the wharf.

A boat was moored near to the steps. A soldier came forward to lift her down and the captain urged her towards it. Two rowers waited. They, too, were obviously men-at-arms wearing no livery to distinguish in whose service they were employed. She staggered and the officer's arm supported her until she was safely seated and Rob clattered down to join her. The captain gave his horse into the charge of one of his subordinates and stepped down. The boatman cast off and the two men on the shore waited until they were mid-stream, then they mounted and made for the Bridge.

She did not attempt to speak with Rob. She knew it would be forbidden and could make matters worse for him. She placed her hand on his arm in token of her gratitude. He looked up and smiled encouragingly.

She had no notion where they were being taken. She did not think it was the Tower, as the King would be unlikely to deal with so unimportant a personage there, some private dwelling would best serve for his business.

The landing steps loomed near and the captain was greeted by two men-at-arms. She was assisted out of the boat and the officer took her arm to lead her across the courtyard. The building seemed enormous, towering dark and menacing over the river.

"Take the other prisoner to the guardhouse. I'll question him later."

Catherine pulled back. "May I speak with him?"

"I'm sorry, mistress, my instructions are to allow you to communicate with no one."

It was as she feared. She said, "God keep you, Rob."

He bowed his head. "Keep a stout heart, mistress. I know you'll do that," and then they hustled him away from her.

Her guard did not seek to mishandle her. He waited courteously then offered his hand again to lead her on.

The room where they left her was in the South Tower. The house seemed vaguely familiar but it was unusually quiet for such an establishment. She was conducted along several stone-flagged corridors, up a flight of stairs and during all the time she saw only one soberly dressed clerk and a nervous young page who stood back from the door when the officer waved him impatiently aside.

The evening shadows were now closing in and as yet the tapers had not been kindled. She stepped in and knew she was alone. She heard the officer speak to the boy outside and he came in, smiled hesitantly, and proceeded to kindle the candles. Now as the furniture sprang into prominence she saw it was a parlour or study. There was a stolid desk by the high window, though it was bare now of papers, an arm-chair, two or three chests. It seemed a pleasant apartment and a fire burned cheerily in the grate, but with it all she felt it was rarely inhabited, as though its owner had left it some years ago and only occasionally was it brought into service. There were no books or any sign of his occupation, no gauntlet or hawking jess, lute or embroidery frame, though she doubted that any lady had worked in this austere chamber.

The boy passed into an inner room and when he returned indicated shyly that she should seat herself and that he would take her cloak. She drew it off reluctantly. Without it she felt in some ridiculous way that she had deprived herself of something of her defences. On the journey she had drawn it tightly round her, as though to keep safe within, her private fears and doubts. Now she felt bereft, vulnerable.

There was no mirror in the room and when the boy left she had to content herself with patting her hair into place beneath the coif and smoothing her crumpled blue silk skirts. She would face her judges as bravely clad and clean as possible. She sat down in the one chair her fingers tightly clasped on her knee to wait.

It seemed an eternity but she knew, in reality, it was no great time and then she heard steps along the corridor and the ring of the men-at-arms' accoutrements. The page's voice came high, deferential. He was very young and the door was opened. She was not facing it and she was determined not to swing round and cringe in terror. She stood and waited till her questioner came to stand behind the table and the clerks, if any were to be allowed attendance, came too with their ink-horns and quills and rolls of parchment.

A voice said quietly, "I was sorry to keep you waiting on my pleasure, Mistress Kingsford."

She went white to the lips as Richard of Gloucester seated himself deliberately behind the desk, waving one hand towards the chair from which she'd risen. The door closed on him. There was no one else, no guard to threaten violence should she insist on keeping silence and no clerk to write down her words.

"My Lord —" she stammered and obeyed him. Why Richard of all men to do the King's bidding in this? Then her mind cleared and she remembered. Was he not Lord Constable of England and empowered to deal with all crimes of treason in the Realm?

He looked very grave, sterner than she had ever known him. There were dark shadows under those grey-green eyes and she was appalled at the marks of suffering clearly betrayed. He had failed then to win mercy for Clarence.

He said, "It took some little time to find you."

"Little enough." Her mouth was suddenly dry. "It seems you must have had prior knowledge of where I would seek refuge."

He inclined his head. "When you failed to return to the palace a search was made. We feared some mischief had befallen you. One of my men questioned the grooms. It seems one was missing. He went to Bankside, they said, to which house they knew not but it was a start."

She looked down numbly at her hands. "My Lord," she said, "I have only one thing to say to you. I regret my part, small though it was, in what has befallen His Grace the Duke of Clarence."

"So you were implicated?"

She swallowed. "We talked of insurrection. How can I deny it since you know it is so? I do not believe it was aught but a vague idea. This latest plot was not of his contrivance."

"I think not." He sounded weary. "It makes little difference now."

"When — when is he to die?"

He raised his head and looked directly into her frightened eyes. "George is dead. It is over."

"I — I don't understand. The execution was not fixed —"

"He died last night in the Bowyer Tower. I have just come from seeing him there."

"Murdered?" Her lips barely framed the word.

"Executed," he corrected gently. "Perhaps it would be unwise to question the manner of it. The Duke is past our help save for our masses for his soul's repose."

"How?" Again her whisper hardly reached him.

"Of poisoned wine, I imagine. The King had given him a butt of malmsey for a Christmas gift. It stood outside his room. He drank from it and died. Whether he was offered that way and chose to take it, since he dreaded the axe, I do not know, or mayhap it was just put in his wine by another. The result was the same. I was assured he did not suffer long."

She began to sob then, great gasping sobs which threatened to tear her in two, and without the solace of tears. He waited as she turned from him, her head bent over the chair arm as she fought for mastery. Then he rose and came to her side, taking her shoulders, twisting her to cry upon his heart.

"Hush, hush, you must not. It can do no good —"

"May God forgive me, I brought him to this —"

"Catherine, that is foolish talk. What childish encouragement you gave him had no effect. This is the result of years of treachery. George, God help him, brought this upon his own head with none to aid him. He ran headlong to his own destruction. He was warned and warned again. He paid no heed. The King has forgiven him more than once. This time it was not possible. Parliament demanded his death, for the peace of the Realm. He went to George himself. He did not leave another to tell him. I think it was then George chose his own way."

Her face hidden against the velvet of his doublet she checked her sobs, as the full horror struck her. There in the Bowyer Tower they had been alone together.

As if she had been present she could picture the scene vividly. Two men, arguing, striking the table, shouting at each other, then the final words, Edward's jovial smile gone for once, his blue eyes cold as North Sea water. Had Clarence tried his final throw? "Send me to my death and I'll speak from the scaffold."

She could not doubt that Edward's handsome mouth hardened then, his fingers clenching and unclenching, those brown, strong fingers she had seen tear a joint asunder, force a fellow combatant's hand flat on the table in friendly bout for mastery. She had given Clarence the knowledge that signed his own death warrant. From that second he had to die. There could be no appeal and no chance of a public scandal. Like the singing boy Clarence had died very quietly.

"I killed him," she whispered piteously.

"What?" He bent his head. "What was it, Catherine? Why do you torture yourself? What lay between you and Edward and Clarence?"

She pulled herself away, her lips parted, eyes as cold as Edward's own.

"What mean you, sir? I have confessed. I was foolish. I talked stupidly of how highly placed I would be if Clarence were King."

"You were his mistress?"

"No."

He shook her shoulder. "Answer me truthfully. Did you bed with him?"

"No — he wanted me. I believe he loved me."

"If he did you were the only being in the whole of his selfish, wasted life he loved."

She said softly, "I think you are right, My Lord. It may be so — for who truly loved *him?*"

Her head was thrown back now in challenge and he dropped his gaze.

"I would have loved him had he let me. I loved him once at Middleham when we were boys and he the elder, stronger, pitied his puny, undersized brother on those rare occasions when he did not taunt and torment him."

She moved from him slightly, one hand on the table.

"I am sorry, sir. I had no right —"

"You felt you had the right to trap my brother in the net of his own vain glory. That was it, wasn't it? You played with us all, and for the same crime. You came to Middleham to sow discord between Anne and I, you married Hugh —"

"I married Hugh because you made me. I had no choice."

He raised his hands in a little helpless gesture and let them fall. "I thought it best."

"It *was* best — for you, My Lord, not for Hugh Kingsford. He fell in love with me."

"And Edward — you played for high stakes there. He took you to his bed."

"Yes." The word was spoken dully and turned from him she did not see the sudden twist of pain contort his lips.

"And you betrayed him with George."

"No, I have told you. My Lord of Clarence never possessed me."

"But Edward believed he did. I was not the only one to seek you today. You have angered the King, Catherine, poured scorn on his manhood. Do you think he can ever forgive you?"

She veiled her eyes with her lashes, keeping her head down-bent, her thoughts racing fast again. Then it was not the King who had ordered her here, and it was not to question her in the King's name that Gloucester had come to her. Then why — ?

"May I — may I sit down, My Lord? I am not well."

"Of course."

She sank down in the chair, forcing her trembling limbs back hard against the struts.

"Others were searching for me — in the city?"

"Aye, King's men and those of My Lord Marquess of Dorset. Are you so stupid, so much a child still that you do not know it deadly to play with fire?"

She said softly, "Why did you send to find me, sir?"

He went from her to the window. "God knows. I have ever considered you my responsibility from the day I found you on the steps of the scaffold in Tewkesbury. There was one dead man near the Abbey wall and another in bad case and you missing. I asked myself why and I learned you had gone to Caxton's shop, unescorted, with only a maid, and she not a woman I would trust, of the Queen's providing, I hear. I could well believe the Queen disliked you but I cannot recall that she ever stooped to murder to rid herself of one of Edward's bedfellows. So again I asked myself who wished Catherine Kingsford dead? Then I knew I must find her first and have her brought here to me."

"Where am I, My Lord?"

He turned, an incredulous smile curving his lips. "You do not know?"

"No. I thought — no matter."

"But you have been to Baynard's Castle before, have you not?"

"I have, but never here."

"This was my apartment before — before my marriage. When in London my mother makes me once more free of it. At present she is at Berkhampstead where she has gone to seek divine aid for George, since her pleas met no response on earthly ears."

She was silent for a moment, then she said, "What is your will concerning me, My Lord?"

He came back from the window to her side. "You are not safe in London — not in England."

Her eyes searched his face.

"You would risk the King's anger?"

"Aye, since I must."

"But how, My Lord?"

"We are on the river. Ships sail from the river, Catherine, and you must be on one as soon as possible."

Panic returned at his danger, cutting across the splendid joy of her discovery.

"It is dangerous. The King may come here. He will ask to see you. It is possible."

He smiled. "It is possible, but Edward is discreet. If he comes he will be told his brother, Gloucester, is busied in his chamber with some light of love. He will not disturb me, nor will he ask to see her. Even affairs of the Realm will not be so highly placed as his consideration of my privacy."

She caught back a little sob and held out her hand, pleadingly, not overclean and dampened with tears.

"My Lord," she said "— My Dear Lord."

CHAPTER XVIII

Her head against his heart, she lay protected in a joy that filled her and separated her from the world outside this room. She knew now he had given back what she had lost at Tewkesbury. From then on she had been bereft. She had moved, talked, acted, but her being had been a shell, formed from the bitter shock of the experience in the market place. Now she was whole, complete, true woman, and her joy was such that she dared not move or speak and break the peace that wrapped and held her safe.

There was no regret that this could be but once. That it had happened was enough. When the dawn light came there would be no tears, recriminations, entreaties. She owed him this at least.

He had been physically and mentally exhausted when he had called for food and they had supped together, so much so, that he had taken little, a leg, a breast of chicken, a cup of wine — no more, and she had eaten because he pressed her and because she would not disobey him in anything.

Even then she had not believed that he would take her. Her throat ached physically from the desire to keep back the words of pleading. Then he had risen and held out his hand. Her fingers had reached out and touched his wonderingly and he had drawn her with him into the bedchamber.

He said quietly, "You should sleep, Catherine."

"No. Don't chide me. Not tonight. I can sleep and sleep after this when I'm alone."

He did not answer and she knew he was frowning and she bit her lip at the thought that she had angered him.

"My Lord, I make no complaint. I wanted nothing but this. You have given me more than I hoped."

He hesitated, then he turned to her and stroked back her hair with his hand. "I cannot explain what I wish without fear of hurting you."

"I know you love her and not me. I do not mind that. I would not hurt her. I love her too."

"That I love Anne does not prevent me from holding real affection for you. Love is not something to be cut up into portions, Catherine. To give to one does not mean that one takes from the other."

"But she would feel betrayed."

"Yes."

"She needs all your love."

"She makes no demands. I am her whole life, I and the boy."

"She will not know from me, I swear it."

He said, "She will not ask and none here would tell her. She accepts my other children without complaint but that was all so long ago and she knows she has no rivals in their mothers."

"Nor in me."

"I want you to find love, Catherine, not to eat out your heart for what cannot be. Edward will soon forget. You will come home. Hugh needs you."

She said dully, "I promised him an heir."

"Is it not what you want?"

"My child would inherit Newburgh. I had comfort in that, but Hugh —"

"Give Hugh time, aye, and yourself."

She smiled. Did he believe time would end her love for him? He did not understand, *could* not. She had given her heart and it would be his always, till he lay in his grave and beyond —

He talked now of his plans for her. "You will have this groom, Wentworth, to accompany you. I have spoken with him and he seems trustworthy. I will choose one other man from my company to go between Burgundy and Middleham with news of you, for I must know you are safe and content. Eventually I wish you to go to Margaret. She will give you a place in her household when I ask it, but first there is a house in Calais where you may stay for a while. I have lodged there on occasions and my servants are reliable and discreet. 'The Rose of London' sails with the tide. I dare not wait for a later vessel."

"When will you leave London?"

"Immediately." His lips tightened. "There is naught to keep me here now. I shall visit George's children tomorrow. I would to God I might take them North with me."

"Will you tell them the truth?"

"Yes. There is naught to be gained in delay. If I do not, someone else will, and perhaps more cruelly. It is unlikely they will know yet. Margaret is a sensible child. She will take it bravely and as for, the boy, I think it will slide over him for a while yet."

She watched him thoughtfully. During the night those tight lines of suffering had eased and though he frowned now in concentration, considering the best means of facing the children, the agony of his grief had faded. Perhaps, like her, he had suffered more because there had been times when he'd wished Clarence dead. She prayed that she had been able to comfort him in some measure.

"My Lord," she said tentatively, "did I — did I please you?"

He sat up abruptly and, reaching down, lifted her chin in his strong brown fingers. "Do you need to ask? Child, were I not wed —" He laughed. "You are so lovely, Catherine and so strong. If it were not I would fear for you — but I don't. You will accept what is, as you have in the past. You have taken on three royal brothers as antagonists and defeated them all in your own way."

"I have not hurt *you.*" She was vehement in her denial but she knew that she had. George's death touched him and she thanked God that even now, he did not know the cause.

He was the heir of England. She thought of the frail, bright boy at Middleham and her heart misgave her. Richard should have other sons but to make the attempt would risk Anne's life and he would not do that. And when the time came and he was alone — for it would come, Catherine had read the signs. She had known too many with Anne's symptoms come to the Convent. They died early as Isobel had. Would he do then what he *must,* take a second bride? She would have given her soul to spare him the heartache ahead.

He bent and touched her cheek lightly. "Tears? Nay, child, you have not hurt me or any of us. What happened did not come from your making. Absolve yourself from blame."

He drew her once more into his arms for comfort and she forgot the day to come and everything but the feel of his lean, hard body against hers and the glory of his kisses.

She had said she would not sleep but she must have done for when he shook her gently awake she saw that the fire had died in the grate and grey light was stealing into the room.

"My Lord, you should rise if Mistress Kingsford is to catch the tide."

A lump formed in her throat as she heard Sir Richard Ratcliffe's quiet, respectful voice beyond the door.

Richard smiled at her encouragingly and reached for his bed-gown.

"Ask the boy to set meat for us. We are coming, Dick."

She tried to eat while he sat at his desk and completed some letters. Then he came to her side more briskly.

"There is gold on board for your immediate needs. More will follow. No" — he checked her anxious refusal — "do not interrupt. Obey me. For once you will accept Yorkist bounty without complaint." He pulled off a ring from his finger and, seizing her hand, pressed it on to her middle finger. "Wear this for added security. I have bought it recently. It will not be missed. Now, come, child, don your cloak for my men are waiting to row you down river before the traffic builds up near the wharves."

She rose and forced her lips to smile.

"Come, kiss me."

He held her close and her fingers reached up and clutched at his jewelled chain, tearing free the small ivory boar of his personal device, Edward's Christmas gift.

"I'm sorry." She held it out pitifully and he smiled.

"Keep it."

"But —"

"Hold it safe for me. I will come with you in the boat. I'd see you safe on board."

She stood on the deck, her fingers clutching the ivory boar, while Rob stood some distance away near the rail. She could not be sure whether the wet on her face was due to the rain and the river mist or tears which would not be held back. It did not matter now for he was too far from her to see.

Below she could hear the noise of the men as they cast off, scurrying to the rigging at their captain's orders, then, at last, when the estuary widened and her longing eyes could no longer distinguish the coast line, she went below. As she entered the small cabin the lant-horn over the doorway which served to lighten the gloom below deck, touched hidden fire from the emerald Gloucester had placed on her finger.

CHAPTER XIX

The sun was warm on her face when she turned from the sea wall towards the ever-watchful Rob; he was waiting discreetly some way away. He never stirred from her side. She smiled. It was May again and an eternity away from the day Gloucester had fetched her from Gupshill.

She had remained secluded in the small house on the quay with Rob to attend her needs and see that she was obeyed by the other servants. Soon she would leave for Burgundy, for even here she was not entirely safe. She had delayed purposely and she would stay for yet a little longer — for now she was sure. At first, when the signs came she had believed that she imagined them, that it was not possible that her dearest wish would be fulfilled. She had gone each day to the Church near the quay and spent long hours staring at the jewelled statue of Our Lady. She was a mother. She would understand and she *had* understood. Catherine would bear a child before The Holy Season of Christmas. The new life within her was so precious she would not risk it yet — for they said the early months were the dangerous ones.

As they entered the hall the French maid-servant curtsied.

"Madame, a messenger has arrived from England. I have put him in the solar."

"Thank you, Louise."

Her heart leaped with hope. He had written. She would know all was well with him. This time she must decide whether she would risk telling him her tidings. Eyes other than his own might read her answer, and it could be disastrous. She must think.

A man turned from the window. She stopped abruptly in the doorway.

"Hugh."

"Catherine."

She flushed like a girl meeting her betrothed for the first time. There was much between them. He came forward and bowed.

"It is good to see you. Are you well?"

"Very well. And you, sir?"

"Certainly."

She said quietly, "You must be angry with me, Hugh."

He smiled crookedly and the familiar scar caught the sun from the window. "My head is firm enough on my shoulders. I am content."

"Did His Grace of Gloucester explain — ?"

"He told me sufficient to make me understand the need for your flight. I warned you of the King's possible reaction to your association with Clarence."

"Yes."

"Well —" He smiled. "All is well."

"You come from Gloucester?"

"Aye."

She moistened her lips nervously. "Have you — have you a letter for me?"

"Aye." He took it from the leathern purse at his hip belt and she fingered the seal but made no move to break it.

"They are all well at Middleham?"

"Yes. Quite well. His Grace has sent me to escort you to Burgundy. He thinks it advisable for me to remain in attendance on the Duchess Margaret and you are to join her ladies. It is all in the letter."

"Oh."

He regarded her steadily. "Will you not sit down, Catherine?"

She came to the armchair and he seated himself on a second near her.

"He commanded me to guard you — naught else, but I would be your true husband, Catherine. How say you? The children are with me, with Nurse and Margery. They are still on board 'The Rose' in harbour. Cecily is impatient to see you."

She would not meet his eyes. She pleated a fold in her skirt nervously. "Would you take me back, Hugh?"

"I love you."

She said, "There are things you must know."

"You did not promise to love me — ever. I accept that. I will not cease to hope that you may come to do so."

"I am to have a child."

"Gloucester's?"

She looked up into his troubled eyes.

"You know?"

"I knew you loved him — that was why you needed to wed me and leave Middleham in such a hurry."

"I would not have you believe he seduced me, Hugh." She threw back her head, proudly. "I wanted him to take me. It will never happen again but I glory in the knowledge that I shall bear his child."

He was silent and she watched him intently. There was no doubt he suffered.

"Have you told him?"

"Not yet. I was not sure."

"Will you do so?"

"I don't know. I would not have the Duchess hurt."

He gave a sigh. "Well, let us pray it will be a son."

"Hugh, if you do not openly accuse me,

that son will inherit Newburgh and Kingsford."

He smiled a trifle wryly. "Yes."

"You would still want me — love me enough to hold us safe from the world, the child and I?"

"Yes." The word was firm enough. "I warn you I shall pray that later you will give *me* a child."

She stood up and went to the window, her eyes wet with tears. Round her neck on a long chain snugly hidden by the embroidered silk of her bodice, Gloucester's white ivory boar nestled against her flesh. She put up a hand to feel its smooth hardness, then she turned back to him.

Richard had talked of his wish that she would find her own happiness and she owed Hugh much.

"Give me time, Hugh," she said quietly and he came forward eagerly to cup her chin in his hands and give her the delayed kiss of greeting.